The Receding Stairs of Oblivion

MALAVIKA KISHORE

First Published in January 2022

ISBN: 978-93-5472-788-7

BLUEROSE PUBLISHERS

www.bluerosepublishers.com

info@bluerosepublishers.com

+91 8882 898 898

Cover Design:

Geetika

Typographic Design:

Namrata Saini

Distributed by: BlueRose, Amazon, Flipkart

Dedication:

For my family and friends with infinite love in their hearts.

Prologue:

"The oldest and strongest emotion of mankind is fear,

And the oldest and strongest kind of fear is fear of the unknown."

- H.P Lovecraft

The Receding Stairs of Oblivion

by

Malavika Kishore

Contents:

Chapter 1

Graduated to Horror Manor

It was two hours past midnight. A new day. But the sun was nowhere to be seen. It was hidden behind the vast, black cloak, sprinkled with shimmering glitter. The silence screeched at a sound much greater than 20 kilohertz. The wind blew so strongly, as if it were to catch the last train to Paris. Fits of laughter were heard in a house in Cormawall.

"To graduation! Cheers!" shouted the whole bunch of them.

"And finally we graduated. The seven of us together. I had reckoned that I would graduate, but who knew about the rest of you?" said Jay with a chuckle.

Bella said, "Save it. Copying off my paper doesn't count."

"Stop this ruckus you guys!" said the rest of them.

Bella's mother, Mrs. Throne, a successful business woman, appeared out of nowhere, and said, "Kids, you've got mail!"

"Okay Ma. Has Uncle Jones called or mailed yet?" shouted Bella.

Mrs. Throne replied, frowning, "Bella, I don't wish to hear anything about your nut-case of an uncle."

Johaneose Jones, the famous psychologist, and detective happened to be Bella's estranged uncle. He was the most famous detective in town, and he also had quite a reputation for his eccentric behaviour. Although Bella's family was not on speaking terms with him, she was his favourite.

"Okay, Let's check the mail, " said Bella.

As she opened the box, she found seven purple Horror Manor tickets glaring at her, and a letter amidst that. Bella read the letter out loud and clear.

"Dear Isabella Throne, Elizabeth Conner, Jay Mousse, Charlie Gray, Graham Lodge, Jane Cooper and Georgie Porter,

I congratulate you on your graduation. You will be pleased to know that as a compliment, I am offering the seven of you tickets to spend a week at the Horror Manor, loved by goosebumps savvy youngsters. It is filled with interesting souvenirs of the grey ghosts and ghouls that roamed the world in the 1st century. I reckoned that you college graduates will be intrigued by these ghastly adventures. I assure you the opportunity to thank me at the end of your trip.

Sincerely,

Your friend MANONYMOUS."

" Wow...This sounds stellar!" exclaimed Georgie.

Suddenly Jane spoke excitedly, "Guys I've heard of this place. It's run by a caretaker called Louis Pinks. Horror enthusiasts like us go there to experience fake paranormal activity, which seems so real. My cousin went there with her chums and I heard that they had a great time. They have deluxe rooms that smell of fresh rose petals and honeysuckle. These rooms face the sea! And the best part is that they have a humongous infinity pool! Even though we don't know who MANONYMOUS is, I suppose that it is safe for us to go there."

"Oh Jane! I can't believe that you said all this in just 10 seconds!" exclaimed Graham.

"I know, right?" replied Charlie.

Georgie shouted, " Hey! What are we waiting for? Let's get to Horror Manor and have a blast!"

"But what about our flight tickets?" asked Bella. Although this might seem like a coincidence, they got an e-mail from MANONYMOUS just that second.

Jay saw it, and exclaimed, "You guys won't believe this! This is from that creepy MANONYMOUS guy again. We're leaving on a private jet to the island, and a boat for us to get to the Horror Manor island from there. Good lord! We leave at dawn tomorrow!"

They shouted jubilantly. Soon they started packing for the grand journey which was only a few hours away.

Finally it was dawn. The most exciting day of their lives. They were going to be on a jet, floating in the orange sky. They said their goodbyes and boarded their very own private jet. Suddenly Jane spoke up, "My intuition tells me that this is going to be the best trip ever. We are going to have the time of our lives! Let the good times roll!"

"Guys, we have time on this jet till sunset. So, to keep us entertained, I have planned this totally marvellous game, called 'The Clue Hunt'. I will give you a riddle and you will 'try' to find the answer to that which will lead you to the next clue and the answer to the third clue is an unexpected one," said Jay.

"Cool!" all echoed, one after the other.

Jay broke the echo by giving out the first clue, "An apple a day keeps the doctor away."

Bella, the smart one, immediately answered, "It's Dr. Lodge. Your Dad, Graham! When we hear the word apple, the first, and only thing that comes to our mind is Sir Isaac Newton, who is the role model of your Dad, who is a doctor."

"Ok now I really think you cheated," said Jay in disbelief. He also added, "The only thing I would have thought of, if I heard apple, would be apple pie. And on that note, your next clue is, 'Dr. Lodge is smart, Dr Lodge is shrewd, but he may sneeze and sneeze, or choke and choke.'

Charlie spoke up, "Hold it right there! I don't need a third clue for this. A dog. That's it. Jay, you may be Dr Lodge's favourite, but what can I say? I'm cooler. Dr Lodge is allergic to dogs, guys!"

"Okay, fine, fine. Here he is!" said Jay. A dog was released from a cabin in the jet, where he was hiding. It was a golden retriever with a shiny gold mane, and dreamy blue eyes. Bella patted it on the head, and gave it a big hug, and said, "Thank you so much Jay! And Graham, thank your Dad for us. I knew he'd have something in store for us, but I most certainly did not expect this cute little guy."

"I knew you'd love it Bella," said Jay, with a cheesy smile on his face.

Betty interrupted, "By the way, I know by what name we should address this sweetheart. Since this is the luckiest day of our lives, on a private jet, I say we call him , Lucky."

"Now I like the sound of that!" exclaimed Georgie, who finally opened his mouth after a very, very long time.

All of a sudden, it started raining cats and dogs. And Bella merrily murmured, "This is really the best day ever." Jay immediately agreed, by giving out a wee little chuckle.

They were extremely euphoric. They deserved to be. Afterall, it was indeed the last day that the seven got to enjoy and cherish together. They were uninformed about the atrocities of the paradise they were about to set foot into. They were not prepared. They didn't know what to expect. It was unbeknown to them that they were digging their own grave.

Chapter 2

At the Horror Manor

Part 1. The Ocean Catastrophe:

It was sundown. The blue canvas had a change of colour to a beautiful sunset orange. The jet was on its wheels again. The seven and Lucky stepped out of the jet and breathed in the fresh air that filled the shore. They immediately took their boat and floated to the island. It was quite a short journey. When they drew closer to the island, they saw the Horror Manor itself, like a humongous castle from the 15th century, made of black bricks in Baker's style. It had dome-shaped tops made of fine crystal. And moreover, the sea was on one side of it, and an infinity pool on the other. From inside the mansion, ran out a stout man with an over-sized pink nose, a patch of grey hair on his head, and a big smile spread across his wide face.

Out of mere excitement, Georgie blurted out, "Are you MANONYMOUS?"

Jane stepped in, to silence Georgie, but the man replied, "MANNY who? I am Louis Pinks and I am the caretaker of this manor. I suppose you are the seven kids my master told me about."

Bella popped a question out of curiosity, "Who is your master, Mr. Pinks?"

"I don't know his name. I have only talked to him by phone. He pays me too. He happens to be a friend of the owner of this place, Mr. Goldson. Allow me to take you to your rooms now," answered Pinks, changing the subject.

When they entered their room, they found themselves in a place bigger than the stadium at their prep-school. Seven beds, neatly laid, were lined up in a row. On the other side of the room, was an indoor heated pool, and a big closet. They were overwhelmed by surprise in an inexplicable way. Pinks said, "Children, this is your dormitory, whilst you stay here." They were quite taken aback, when they heard him say that. Even Lucky's eyes became really wide, out of surprise. But only Jay with his utterly puerile behaviour (which Bella completely abhorred), cared to ask Charlie, "Dude, did you hear the guy? He just called this luxury suite a dormitory. I guess he doesn't know a better word." He then gave out a weird little chuckle, and Bella snorted at him. And then, Pinks told the children, "You are here after a very tiring journey, I presume. So why don't you rest while I make you a simple seven-course dinner!" After hearing this, it looked like the seven were going to drool after imagining eating a 'simple' seven-course dinner.

They had their dinner, and Lucky settled in a large corner of their room. All of them went to bed. Very soon, it was midnight. The hound of Horror Manor (they had a hound like all the other creepy manors around the globe) started howling. Six of them were sound sleepers, but not Bella.

She got up, still trying to figure out who MANONYMOUS was. She told herself, "He had written in the letter that we would get a chance to thank him at the end of the trip. So it means that he will be coming here. So……"

At that very moment, she heard a sound, "Thud!" She turned back to her bed-side window. And what she saw was despicable. It was a ghoulish figure knocking at her window. Its flesh was rotting, and its eyes were hollow. She had never seen anything like it. She felt like she was on the verge of blacking out, and gave out a shrill scream. That was enough to wake the others. They were startled. And when she pointed at the window to show the ghoul to the others, it had vanished. Bella was not one who believed in the existence of evil spirits and ghoulish antagonistic zombies. But what she saw was true. Or maybe not. But when she told the others about her brush with horror, they consoled her. Lucky ran towards her and cuddled in her lap. Betty said, "Bells, you are one of the bravest people I know of. It could have just been a hallucination of some sort. It was indeed an exhausting trip, and you're not exactly the soundest sleeper. Or it might even be a fake horror trick. It is Horror Manor after all."

Then Jay said, "Yup that's enough for today people. Everyone, bed. Now."

The next morning, they woke up on hearing Lucky bark. He was barking at the closet. "That's strange. We never even opened that closet. Then why is Lucky barking at it?" asked Bella. Lucky did not seem to stop. They decided to open the closet. And when they did, they saw the exact same ghoulish figure that Bella had described to them last night. Jay tried to hit it with a suitcase. Jane, Graham, Charlie and Betty screamed in such a way that their voice shook the gigantic mansion. Georgie passed out. But Bella just stood there, staring. Mr. Pinks entered the room at that very moment, wishing them good morning, but saw them with the ghoul. Then he said, "That's enough Barry. Come out of that ghastly robe. You scared them to death." The ghoul revealed itself by pulling off the rotten face mask.

Jay remarked, "It's a guy! A normal dude. Is this one of those fake horrors which are part of our trip?"

Pinks replied, "Yes. Indeed. But the real horror starts today."

Once they had their delectable breakfast which consisted of waffles, pies, and date tarts, the group headed to the Horror Ocean for their very first adventure. Pinks explained, "Now now, gather around here kids, and mutt. This is the Horror Ocean. You needn't fear because the ocean current is calm and it is not too deep. You may be intrigued by many things that you are going to see underwater. I will be cleaning Mr. Goldson's suite, right inside the Manor. Anything you might require, do not hesitate to call me. Have fun! And also please avoid going westward. The tide there is extremely high."

Bella shouted, "Oh! Wait Mr. Pinks! Why are you cleaning his room? Is he currently living there?"

"Oh! No. His friend, my master, will be arriving at the end of the week," replied Mr. Pinks, walking towards the Manor.

Lucky lay down on the sand, his tongue hanging out because of the scorching heat.

They jumped into the ocean. And when they reached the ocean floor, the colour of the ocean changed from greenish-blue to black. Thick, dark black. Then something was shimmering. A school of giant piranhas. Of course it was not real. There were people under those costumes too in the fake sea. The fish chased them around. While the others were swiftly swimming, Graham was being chased by a ghost mermaid. He was being chased westwards. The others were enjoying themselves. But unbeknownst to them, Graham was struggling in that thick black rising water. He gasped for breath, while the others came ashore. And very soon, he was sucked into the blues, or might we call it the blacks of the ocean. The rest of them started walking back to the Manor, thinking of the wonderful experience they had. Suddenly, Betty remembered, "Wait! Where is Graham? Didn't he swim back up?"

It was then that they realized that Graham was missing. They ran to the sea-side. Jay jumped into the water to search for him. But they couldn't. The machine-generated tide was too strong. Jay had to return without Graham. They called for Pinks. He consoled them, "Graham might have made it to the other shore. This has happened to many visitors. When the tide rose, he might have swum to the next shore. He'll return by tomorrow morning."

They waited by the shore for the rest of the day. Time flew by, with the wind. But Graham never returned. They didn't lose hope. They waited. All night long.

The next morning was similar to the last. Except, the person who screamed was Jane, and it sounded much worse. At least Bella was screaming about a living person. Not a dead, cold one. When the others woke up, they screamed too. When Mr. Pinks came down from the high manor to the shore, where all of them spent the night waiting, and he consoled the others, "The poor boy was misfortunate. I am really sorry. Seemed like a good chap."

Graham's body had washed ashore sometime back. The body, if it could be called a body at this point, was mutilated. There were marks of all sorts of weapons on his "body". A slight tug would be enough to dismember it. He'd lost a lot of blood. He looked pale. And in some parts, the skin was absent too. Peeled off, to be exact. His face wasn't too recognizable either.

For a few hours, all that was heard from the isle, was weeping. It echoed through the island. Charlie spoke, " Guys, we must call our parents. Arrange a funeral. And leave this place."

"No, wait! He made it to the shore. It was murder. A cold-blooded murder," said Bella.

Jay inquired, "How come? If he made it to the shore, who killed him?"

"I don't know who, but I think I know how. I'm guessing, when he reached the shore, someone who didn't want him there, a madman, tried to kill him. Look at him. He's been mutilated."

Bella was right. The detective in her had exemplary intuition. But three unanswerable questions remained. Who? Why? Is one of them a witness, or more probably, a psychotic killer?

Part 2. Scared to The Core:

There's something about fear. Fear is like a tornado. And when it strikes, it brings everyone together, in one place. Frightens them. If it's strong enough, it can make even the brave kneel. What could be stronger than a homicide?

They packed their stuff, and the six and Lucky got ready to leave the place with Graham's cold, lifeless body. They told Pinks, "We are leaving now. We haven't told our parents yet, because if they knew, they would come here to get us, putting themselves in danger. This place is cursed. And you better get out of here too."

Pinks replied, "My apologies, but you cannot leave. A storm has struck Cormawall and the islands nearby, including this one, and the sea is no longer safe for a boat ride. It will all be back to normal within two weeks. You can't contact anyone. The phone signals are blocked. I suppose you will have to stay here till then."

That was it. Their final chance to leave the island was gone. They were sure that they were trapped in the chamber of death. Death had opened the door for them, and they had wilfully entered. Not thinking about the consequences. It was time, but they had some courage left.

There was a burial. It was not a cliché, like the wonted one with a priest blurting out hymns, or with mourning people, half of them who didn't even know the dead man in the coffin. But it was at midnight. Their third night at Horror Manor. And Lucky was howling too. Usually, people would mourn the death of their loved one, whilst at a funeral, but here they didn't even shed a tear. They were thinking. All of them. They were thinking about the same thing. Fighting crime. Investigating the murder of their dear chum, while they might be victims, or murderers.

They spent the whole of next morning in their room. Thinking about what to do. And suddenly, Bella spoke, "We are trapped here. For good. Now the only thing left for us to do, is to find the killer. His motive. Pinks can also be suspected. In fact, every one of us is a suspect."

Jay said, "I suggest we search Pink's room. Look out for anything suspicious, like a gun or a knife."

They marched over to Pinks' room while he was out cleaning Goldson's room. They started their search. But they were unsuccessful in their quest. And when they were about to exit the room, Bella's sharp eye caught something. A radio. Which was probably used by Pinks to contact the boat and airline services to know about the storm. And something crossed her mind. She shouted, "Wait! A radio! That's it!"

The others looked at her blankly. She explained, "Detectives use the police radio frequency to know if a crime has taken place, and to get hold of the details which may be useful for them in the case. I remember seeing Uncle Jones sit by the radio every morning at around 10:00 am when he was living with us. It's almost 10:00 am. We must tune in, to the frequency he listens to, and try and talk to him. Ask him for help."

The others agreed. What else could they do? They tuned into the police radio frequency, hoping that Jones would hear them. Bella spoke into the radio, "Uncle Jones, Bella here. Trapped in Horror Island. Help!"

Jones was currently living in the countryside near Cormawall. Just as Bella assumed, he was sitting next to his radio at 10:00 am. He told himself, "Jones, you will be lucky, at least today, to get a thrilling case to crack." At that very second, he heard Bella's voice. What he wished for had come true. On hearing what Bella had to say, immediately he tried booking a boat ticket, but it was all blocked because of the storm. But what could he do? He had to help Bella. The only person he considered family.

Having no other alternative, he called his sister, Ansy, and rented a small ferryboat, to get to the island. Ansy Olson Throne, better known as, Ansy O. Umnom, was in the export business with her spouse Jake Umnom. They both took the name of their lucrative company. The Umnom Industries owned a chain of boats, but Jones never thought of seeking help from his own sister, because of the shattered relationship he shared with his family. But he maintained contact with Ansy, until he left for Alaska, years back. He was warned of the fast approaching storm and was asked to take the Umnoms' private trade route to the island.

He packed whatever that he thought would come in handy, and sailed away.

It was noon, and they were all taking a walk in the sun. It was supposed to be relaxing, as they were at the beach. But all they could think of, was about Graham, his killer, and an all-pervasive thought that the blood-thirsty killer was going to be murdering them all, in that horrendous island.

Bella and her friends struggled to find some solace. They had hope. And their hope didn't fail them.

While walking, Georgie spotted something. A boat. And someone in it. He shouted, "Guys, a boat!"

And when everyone turned back to look, the boat had almost reached the shore. Bella screamed happily, "Uncle Jones!" She ran across the blue waters and gave him a hug.

"How I've missed you dear. The last time I saw you was ages ago. Tell me clearly how you ended up here. My my! isn't this a horrific place? And they call this adventure. And are they your friends?" said Detective Jones, with his strange parlance and demeanor, to which the others grunted.

Bella answered by introducing them to Jones, "Uncle, they are my friends from college. At the night of our graduation, we got a strange mail from a guy named MANONYMOUS, who is Graham's potential killer, and he sent us tickets to this place, as a gift. We got excited, and made the mistake of coming here."

"What kind of mindless idiots are you all? Exhibiting such uncanny behaviour? Bella, are you not my niece? Didn't you feel an ounce of queerness when some unknown man sent you tickets to such a hideous place?" scolded Jones. They blandly glared at him, succumbing to all his whining and shouting.

After a minute, Pinks entered and inquired, "Forgive me for my rude behaviour, but who are you, and where did you come from?" Jones started giggling away, as if he had smelled laughing gas. He answered back, continuing to laugh, "What a funny caretaker! Just hilarious. I'm an incredibly famous detective and you might not know me, because I spent half my career in Alaska, where I had a wonderful job. I retired, and now I am a private detective who still uses the police radio frequency as a method to communicate with people and understand their troubles. My niece here, Bella, was intelligent enough to tune in and ask for my help before it was too late. Even though you people wouldn't be able to travel at the time of such a terrifying storm, I have my ways."

All of them were now popping their eyes out on hearing the way the man talks, but Bella was smiling as if she admired this trait of his. She asked, "How did you know that he was the caretaker?"

"My dear, it's just observation, which you may gain only after very much experience. He is wearing an apron, and not only that, it is a cliché that caretakers usually look like this," explained Jones.

Pinks scowled, while the others giggled. He said, "Let me show you to your room, Sir."

Georgie told Bella, " No offense, Bella, but your dear old uncle is a snob."

The others laughed at Georgie's remark.

Time flew by, and it was sundown. They were all sitting in the garden, while Pinks served them exotic hibiscus tea. Betty remarked, "This is heavenly." The others agreed. Just as Lucky liked Bella, he got close to Jones too. They were very much akin.

While the others were blowing their tea to get it to a lukewarm state, Jones was whistling away, which made Jay ask, "Why are you doing that?"

He replied, “When you whistle onto the tea, it gets cooler much faster than your medieval methods.”

Jay sighed, and said, “So, let's come to the point. Can you help us get out of this island, and get hold of this killer before he kills us too?”

“What a question! There has never been a case that I couldn’t solve. Except one. Now, moving on. So Bella tells me that the boy, Graham, was swimming, and due to the tide he might’ve swam to the next shore, and also that he was cut up very badly. I would have taken you back with me in my boat, but this killer might just follow us back.”

“How can you be so sure?” questioned Jane.

“Experience. Just mere experience. The man or woman living in that uninhabited island, the potential killer, obviously has a motive. So, we can hereby say that he is vengeful, for an unknown reason. And since he took the trouble of getting you tickets to this place, he wouldn’t mind following you kids back to Cormawall, if you return at all,” said Jones.

Bella said to Pinks, “Mr. Pinks, you said that your master would return at the end of this week right?”

“I’m afraid not. Because of the storm, he will not be able to come. He also stated that he wouldn’t have to visit you all,” said Pinks.

Charlie questioned frighteningly, “Does that mean that we’ll be dead by then?”

Chapter 3

A Gist of the Past and a Tyrannical Investigation

Life is like a kite. The strings are in one's hands. Pull the right string, and the kite will soar, in the sky, and into the beyond. But what could Bella and her friends possibly do? They had opened a Pandora's box. In which hid, a mysterious killer, with a mysterious motive, which had to be investigated, by none other than Detective Jones, their only potential saviour.

The night swept away really fast. It was the beginning of their fifth day at Horror Manor. Lucky, and five of them were snoring away. But Bella was up. So was Jones. She walked to his room, to find him sipping away his green tea. That was what Jones usually did, when he was figuring out a problem. She asked him, "Good morning. Thinking about something?"

"Oh! Not important. I was just missing Celia," said Jones.

Bella queried, "You're missing mom? I have never actually wanted to know, but why doesn't the rest of our family speak to you? Not even my mother."

"Ok. I suppose it's time to tell you now. It all began 17 years ago. I had just started working as a junior detective, your Auntie Ansy was starting her own business, and your Mom was an established business woman by then, and you were an adorable little pre-schooler. Things were going well, until I got a strange case. Our town was pretty small back then. No one really enquired about things a lot. It was small enough to be the perfect place to commit a murder. More precisely, a chain of murders. Since I was the only junior detective, I had to be part of that case."

Bella suddenly posed a question, "Wait! Like a serial murder? Did our town ever have serial killers?"

Jones continued, "It was actually the first time and the last, that a serial killer painted the town with murder. Now, let me continue. That particular killer was known as The Artist. He or she would slay his victim, and would cut up his fingers, use it to paint a canvas, and would leave it at the crime scene. The killer was known like that, because they murdered people who were corrupt business-practitioners, and planted the bloodied canvas there, probably to show the intensity with which revenge was taken on them. The most brilliant criminal I have ever seen to date. They left no evidence. None at all. I did a lot of digging, and found out the bitter truth that Celia is a suspect."

"What? My Mom? But she's so sweet. And I am certain that she would never do such a thing. Why did you even suspect her? Was she arrested? Was she The Artist?"

Bella was shocked about the fact that her Uncle would do such a thing.

Jones spoke solemnly, "Of course not! Your mother was not a murderer. Why on earth would you think that? I just had a mere suspicion. She had known all the victims, as our family was in business with them, and was on the verge of being bankrupt. She was an excellent painter, and had so many of those canvases, that we found at the crime scenes. Every day a murder was committed, one of her canvases always went missing. As a detective, I had to do my job. I had to suspect her, even though I knew my sister really well. As a result of my misapprehension, I was kicked out of the house, and Celia said that she never wanted to see me again. It was indeed the worst day of my life. Not only that, but also, the identity of The Artist remains a mystery to date. We closed the case as the killer broke the chain, and stopped when all the corrupt businessmen in town were dead. I have never seen Celia or anyone else in my family since then. Ansy used to call sometimes, to see how I was doing, until I shifted to Alaska, where I finally found some peace, and time to get over my guilt. The only other contact I had was you. You and Ansy never loathed me. I still wonder why."

Bella was almost starting to tear up. She said, "I'm so sorry. I understand. You were a detective. You had no other option. Although Mom and Dad always spoke badly about you, you were my role model. You still are."

Jones was also teary eyed, after Bella spoke those words. He said, "I want to help you and your friends out of this web of crime and homicide. Let's let go of the past, and focus on the case of Graham's death, and furthermore, MANONYMOUS."

It was almost 9 am when the morning light stroked their faces. Since Bella and Jones were already up, they cooked the others some eggs and bacon. After having their breakfast, they sat around the dining table, to listen to what Jones was going to say. Jones began, "We are playing a game of hide and seek. I will be seeking evidence, proof, or whatever that leads us to finding out the whereabouts of the killer. And every single person on this isle, or even the next, will be equally suspected, including myself. Jay chimed in, "So what do we have to do? Get alibis? Interrogate everyone?"

"Exactly! So let's get started with the interrogation. Why don't we begin with the caretaker?"

The astute detective and the six graduates walked out of the Manor, to find Mr. Pinks basking in the morning sun. He was taking time off work, to relieve his so-called stress. Jones said, "Good morning Pinks! I am starting my investigation today, and I would like to begin with you. Tell me a little something about yourself, your master, and the owner of this place. Also pray for your alibi to not be completely foolish, that is, if you have one."

"Okay. I am Louis Pinks. I am 53, and I have been living here, serving visitors at this Horror Manor for about 25 years. The owner of this place , Mr. Goldson, who is currently out of the country, is one of my two masters. My second master is anonymous to me, as I have only heard the first one talk about whoever the second one is."

"If you don't know the person, how is he or she your master? And your alibi?" questioned Jones.

Pinks replied with a sigh, "He pays me for having you here as guests, and for taking care of your needs and making you feel comfortable. That's how he is my master. And you can ask the kids, they saw me go into the Manor, to clean my master's room, thinking that he would be coming. But he will not be turning up, due to the storm."

"Ok. I will call for you if I have a query. Thank you Pinks!" said Jones. Pinks walked away with a scowl spread across his face.

Bella asked, "Now who, Uncle Jones?"

"Now I want the other workers," said Jones, with his face gleaming in the sunlight.

Jones, and the young detectives were extremely keen to investigate every nook and corner of the Horror Manor, and to try and get the ruthless killer out of their lives.

Jones started interrogating the workers. They all looked nervous. They stammered like hens. But after all that hard work, all Jones heard was, "Oh my! A murder? Pinks didn't even bother to tell us. We were all under water at the time your friend died. Each and everyone of us was. We were not allowed to come to the shore, until your show was over. Lest, we should not get our pay. Our master said so. Now please leave. We only know so much."

Jane said, "Mr. Jones, they are not willing to answer. Now what should we do?"

"Do not worry Jane, the truth has a way of coming to us. This is only the first part of my investigation. The workers are not important. You are. Now I will be critically interrogating you. I will analyze my studies, and I hope to give you some crucial information today.

"So Bella, since you were all together when the boy died, you can answer for the six of you, Okay?" said Jones.

"Sure," answered Bella.

Jones began.

"When did you all notice that Graham went missing?"

"We were being chased by the piranha people, and I noticed Graham being chased by one of the ghost mermaids. They were all about. I think he accidentally swam towards the higher current area, and we didn't see him afterwards. We only realized, when we got to the shore," said Bella, her glasses starting to fog up. "Ok. But how come none of you jumped back into the fake ocean, or whatever, to rescue your friend? Doesn't that evidently show that you had an agenda all along? That you wanted him to die?" shouted Jones.

Jay scolded, "How dare you speak like this? Are you saying that we killed him? For what? He was our friend. A good person. Why would we ever want him to die? For what reason? You're nuts."

"I am a detective. Not a nanny. I have to be critical and careful in my investigation. I don't feel any sympathy for you. For you might be murderers. All of you," said Jones.

"Uncle! We would never. Please believe us! We don't even have a motive. Please stop this. I don't think this is the way to go about this," Bella screamed her lungs out.

Suddenly, someone started screaming. It was coming from the beach. They ran straight out of the mansion. When they reached the shore, they saw a crowd of workers, and the howling Lucky, standing around something. They ran past the crowd, pushing them aside. They saw a mutilated body. But it was quite recognizable, just like Graham was. It was none other than Louis Pinks. He was brutally murdered. The killer, whoever it might've been, ripped off his skin with a knife. At least it looked like that. Whoever did it, was the vilest person Jones, or anyone for that matter, could possibly know. The killer was true evil. But who could it be? One of the workers? The six other college graduates? Jones? Were they supposed to track the murderer down, for what their lives were worth? Or the more probable question could be, would they have to track themselves down?

Chapter 4

The Excavation, Perambulation Scheme

Another funeral was on. It was a pretty quick procedure. A burial, and a howl sponsored by Lucky. After the funeral, the gathering was dispersed. The workers had no more chores left to do. The bleak Manor stood still throughout an extremely heavy thunderstorm. When the six guests of death saw each lightning, and heard each thunder, their hearts took a leap. It seemed as if death drew closer. The surging waves approached as if they were going to gobble up the Manor, and its residents. Technically, it didn't matter, because they were going to be gobbled up soon. By none other than death. So, the million dollar question was: Who was going to be next?

"I have to save the children. And myself. But how? Such a strange case? There must be some sort of a loophole. Somewhere. As of now, it seems as if it's in the midst of nowhere," Jones said to himself in his mind. Suddenly, interrupting his sober thought, Bella asked, "I have a question. Why did you question us like that the other day?

You were not yourself. Is there anything that you are hiding from us?"

Jones sighed, "I knew you would understand. You are just like me, Bella. We have the same thoughts, intuitions. I just wanted to make sure that you were not keeping anything from me. You see, I've learnt, as a psychologist, that normally, a suspect, who is actually a criminal, reacts in a quite peculiar way. Earlier, when I accused you of murder, and that too, of your dear friend, all of you got emotional. You didn't sweat, you didn't get nervous. You just shouted helplessly. Teary-eyed. Usually, an innocent suspect, free of guilt, would get angry and upset really fast. An intelligent criminal would have understood that I would not be able to suspect anyone, based on the information I have. I hadn't even begun questioning you, when I accused you. A criminal would act cool, as he or she would know that I was faking it."

Bella's eyes popped out of her specks. "But there can be exceptions, right?"

Jones replied, smiling, "That's right. But I hid something from you. The ocean you went to was not real. It was more like a huge water ride in an amusement park. Without telling you, I explored the place a little, and demanded Pinks of the CCTV footage, featuring the Horror Ocean, and its coasts. You missed the point that the ocean wasn't real. In a proper adventure park, or whatever this is, would have cameras near every ride. And so did this death ride. And coming to the point, when I checked the footage, I saw all of you coming out without Graham, getting nervous, trying to save him, and crying helplessly. I was just making sure, by questioning you."

"You're unbelievable, Uncle," said Bella, smiling in satisfaction.

Jones sighed. "We lost a crucial lead in this case. If only Pinks were alive, we could have gotten more info and whereabouts of his so-called masters. As I noticed, he was a very loyal servant. He might've seen his master, but to protect him, he probably fooled us by sternly saying that he had never seen that man. He might've paid him good cash for it. However, there is no point in whining about it now."

Bella curiously asked, "If he was loyal, why would his master, or masters, murder and mutilate him?"

"He might've acquired insider information about them, or might've seen or heard too much. A man like Pinks is very easy to manipulate. By giving him wads of cash, they possibly made him do all their dirty work," Jones answered.

Bella chimed in with ideas.

"Maybe they asked Pinks to do something he didn't want to, he refused, and so, they killed him."

"Possible. But we can't be sure of anything yet. Now surely, Pinks didn't murder Graham. I don't think he ever had the stomach for an assassination," replied Jones.

Bella stated, "But we can never be sure. He had the time to get to the other shore..."

"That's it! Bella dear, we missed out something. The other island! We never thought of going there to look for clues. Evidences! If he was murdered there, the killer must have left behind some trails at least."

Jay cut in. "Are you nuts? Do you intend to get us all killed? Right after you accused us? No way!"

"It was just part of my investigation. Bear with me, or never find your friend's killer. We are going to that island right now," Jones scolded.

"But Mr. Jones, that island is uninhabited. How do you expect a killer to live there?" Jane asked.

"What more of a luxury does an assailant require? An isolated workspace, a place to store arms, acres of burial ground, and also, it is not very tough to acquire canned food for a week or two."

Bella gasped and said, "Woah! Uncle, are you proposing an excavation? Like a patrol?"

Jones replied, "Essentially, yes."

Jay didn't look convinced. But said, "Fine, Sherlock ! But if you plan on accusing us, trapping us, or trying any of your queer antics on us, we'll return home. And if you happen to suddenly discover something fishy or even suspect us secretly, try not to get all Freddy Krueger with us. As of now, I really don't care if I am going to spend the rest of my life in a coffin!"

"I will only tell you my suspicions, if at all I have any. Don't take them seriously. I would never trap my niece and her chums. And don't even think about going back home with a psycho killer tagging along. So, let's get going! And by the way, never address me with names of fictional detectives, or with ridiculous lunatics having lower intellect than I do. Not even sarcastically! And if you do, you will soon find yourself seeing your life go by in this godforsaken island."

Bella had no alternative, but to laugh.

Chapter 5

The Shadow of a Doubt

'Life is not an Agatha Christie novel. It's a lot messier,' said Jughead Jones. Although it was just a quote, it actually proved meaningful in Bella and her friends' case, for what was about to come next.

Trust has two meanings. One of them is to believe in whatever a person says or does. To trust that person with one's life. Well, the other is to believe whatever a person 'claims' to have done. Both are entirely different. But in that very rare, particular case, there were no options. In fact, the killer had provided them with no options. They had to trust what they had in hand, even when it was improbable, or even impossible.

Mornings are supposed to be very calm and serene. But Bella's doubt disrupted the peace and quiet of their seventh morning at the "Death" Manor. She was standing on the balcony. Her hazy blue eyes pierced through the sky. Jones came out too. He asked, "What are you thinking about?

A new idea? A lead? A doubt?"

Bella sighed. "Yes, Uncle. But I'm positive that it is only a doubt. It should be. Or else, no one is sane anymore."

"Tell me," said Jones, in his calm and consoling voice.

"It's merely a shadow of a doubt. But Uncle Jones, I have to ask, do you think The Artist is dead? Or that he stopped killing people?" Bella said.

Jones looked surprised. "My dear, why would you ask that, in this context? Do you think…."

"As I said, just a doubt," Bella said abruptly.

Jones had to ask, "But why?"

"It's just that, Uncle, were you sure about The Artist's motive? Because I'm not. Just look, it's just my intuition, but you told me that our town's only killer, murdered people who were corrupt businessmen. But, there is one reason why he could have murdered Graham. He didn't get any good placement opportunities after graduation. So, umm, he kind of had his father pay his company's head, to give him a better post. His boss is Dr. Lodge's friend. Graham's Dad, who is also part businessman, becomes corrupt this way. Doesn't that give him a motive?"

Jones spoke, "You have a good theory there. And yes, there were no corrupt businessmen left in town, after the final one's demise, 17 years ago. But don't you think what you said is quite vague? What are the odds of The Artist, who might even be dead by now, to know your friend's pop so well, to even know insider information about his doings? And anyway, one logical question is, why didn't this assailant, murder his father, who is the actual 'corrupt businessman'? Why did he murder Graham? I am pretty sure that he is not a teen accomplice. The Artist's pattern is different. He would have murdered the actual sinner."

"Yeah. I guess so," said Bella, not entirely satisfied.

Jay and the rest of the crew walked up to them, "Mr. Jones, Bella, what are we supposed to do?"

Jones said, "We are going on that very excavation trip that we planned yesterday. We're going to the other island. Where we believe, Graham and Pinks were murdered."

The others had to agree. It was actually the only way that they could find a lead.

They were going to search every nook and corner of that "uninhabited" island. To find a lead. Or even better, to find the killer.

The storm was subsiding. But no boats arrived for them. They had to borrow sleeping bags from the workers, to float over the fake Horror Ocean, to reach the uninhabited hell.

And so they did.

The shores looked much akin to the Horror Island's shore. But the only difference was that there was no manor, no breeze, and no people.

Charlie exclaimed, "I bet on my life that this place is uninhabited. How on earth can anyone live here?"

Jones smiled grimly. "People like us can't. But a killer, desperate to claim the lives of his victims, most certainly can."

That gave them the creeps.

They started their search. For nothing in particular though.

Betty asked curiously, "What are we supposed to look for?"

Bella replied to that, looking at her Uncle for approval, "Knives, blood, a shelter, food cans, or something to prove that Graham and Pinks were here. Or at least Graham. We are not sure of Pinks dying, or being murdered here."

Jones nodded in approval. "I see a future detective when I look at you, my dear."

Bella smiled, thinking of how amazing it would be, to crack cases. To join a detective squad. Just like Uncle Jones. But all those were the things that were not exactly in the foreseeable future. They were only happening if they returned home, well and alive.

They searched. Searched. And searched. Bella and her friends did not lose hope. They were sure to find something. Just then, Bella heard a creak in the woods.

Chapter 6

An Angel from Heaven

Sometimes, what we see in front of us, is not what it seems to be. Sometimes, it might be an angel in disguise. Flown down right from heaven. But the other times, it can be an angel of death from hell. Or to make matters even worse, Satan himself might just arrive.

Bella turned back to see what it was. She was expecting a savage killer, ready to assassinate her. But on the contrary, it was a seagull that might've flown in from somewhere. But for them, it was their saviour. An angel in disguise! Who would've thought that the gull would find the lead?

It didn't strike the others, but it sure did strike the Uncle and niece.

Bella screamed, "Oh my god, guys! The seagull! It's eating out the leftovers from a food can! Which means….."

Jay finished her sentence ,"Time to follow the crumb trail," to which the others beamed.

They walked. Finally, they reached a stop. A place that looked like a garage. Bella went forward to pull it open.

And she did. What they saw, was the unthinkable. There was a shady-looking man. Dead. Cold. Mutilated. They found something else in extra. A bloodied canvas! Georgie and Jane screamed in horror! The others froze in time.

Jay suddenly spoke, "Mr. Jones, what do we do?"

Jones replied coldly, "We have to inform the cops, regardless of the storm. We have to return to our town, and continue our investigation there. Clearly, the killer left for town before us. We have to return home. Have I made myself clear?"

Betty said, lifting an object from the ground, "Mr. Jones, look at this. A suitcase. It's probably this man's." Charlie took the suitcase from her, and searched it thoroughly. All they saw were some documents, and an ID.

Betty suddenly gasped, "Mr. Jones, I know this man. He was a friend of Graham's Dad. I saw him when we visited his house. He is a renowned businessman. Claudius McKinsley. That's what Dr. Lodge told me when I asked. That they were doing business together. He didn't tell me what business it was. He said that it was highly classified."

Jones said, "Bella, your intuition strikes again!"

The others looked at Jones blankly. Just then, Bella said, "Guys, about 17 years ago, we had a serial killer in our town, called The Artist, with a sinister motive of killing all the corrupt businessmen in town. He completed his mission. That's what we thought. Until...."

Charlie chimed in, "So you are saying that The Artist is striking again? That he is finishing what he started back then? So Graham's Dad is corrupt too? How could he?"

"But I have a doubt. If Dr. Lodge is the corrupt person, why was Graham killed? Why?" Betty asked.

Jones said, "To that, I have no answer. But I will give it to you. I will end this. But I need your help. We have to trust each other. Or else, the assailant can use it against us. From what I saw, he or she is keeping tabs on us. For sure."

They returned to Horror Island, possibly, or hopefully for the last time. They packed up all over again, and used the radio to inform the cops. The police were going to send over boats to pick them up. They were all so eager to leave, except Lucky, as he had adapted to life in the isle. But they somehow coerced him to come. The boats drew nearer, and they jumped into them. They were all sitting in those boats, set to steal their livelihood back from the Grinch.

Chapter 7

Home Sweet Home

Hope is not just a feeling. It is freedom. Freedom to think about whatever solution one desires, regardless of the reality. Whatever Gordian knot is tied in between one's life, hope does not depend upon it. Whatever it may be. Even when there are multiple knots tangling one's life. Take Jones and the graduates' case for instance. They were fighting an epic battle against an executioner with a toxic psyche, who could actually be a potential former serial-killer. He had managed to take the lives of so many in the past. What are the odds that he would spare them?

What a cliched phrase, 'home sweet home' is. In wonted cases, people would be happy that they finally reached home. A home is a haven, which screams out happiness and comfort. A place that everyone, without exception, misses, or longs for, at least once, when away and beyond. But how was there even a remote chance that Bella and the team must feel the same? How were they supposed to say 'home sweet home' when they saw their homes, even though after long, when there would be a terminator at their doorstep, waiting to say 'MISSION

ACCOMPLISHED'? The answer was crystal clear. They couldn't. Not in a millennium.

After a fleeting hiatus, Jones, Bella, and the others reached the façade of the Throne Residence. The luxurious abode of the Throne family, consisting of Mr. and Mrs. Throne, their housekeeper Holly, and Bella's bedridden Nana Throne, who were awaiting the arrival of Bella and her 'six' friends. Little did they know that they were supposed to host three unexpected guests too.

They were all received by their parents, together in Bella's home. Their initial intention was to welcome their sons and daughters as soon as they came, in merry surprise. But they never imagined to hear what was about to come out of their mouths.

Dr. Lodge asked, his beam fading from his face, "Where's my boy? Where is he?"

"Why in God's name is this man here? He accused me, took on a new name Jones, and left. For good. Why is he with you kids? This man is considered estranged by our family. Come in and explain yourselves. Everyone!" yelled Mrs. Throne, taken aback by the turn of events.

Every ominous thing has a silver lining. Just like that, every gracious and pleasant thing always has a sinister, rotting side. When one's happiness grows, a vicious parasite starts biting every bit of it from the other, unseen end. The children's parents had been too excited to hear about their time at the Manor and its supposedly awesome features and beauties. They expected that trip to be a fun graduation trip, right before going to earn, doing their niche jobs. But in the midst of all that joy, they had forgotten to prepare themselves for the worst, and beyond.

They all sat inside the Throne Residence, around their humongous lounge. The maid, Holly, got them peach pies and noodle salads, for them to feel fresh after their tedious journey.

Mr. Throne spoke, "Begin…."

Bella said, "Dad, we lied."

"Whatever do you mean?" said Bella's father, his face becoming even more sober.

Bella continued, "A week ago, when we left for the trip, we got mail, right? It is probably from a fake address. We actually don't know who sent us the mail. The only information that we have is that he is the owner, Mr. Goldson's friend."

Mr. Lodge interrupted angrily, "Stop your ruddy blabbering and tell me where my son is!"

Bella couldn't bring herself to say that to Dr. Lodge. She looked blankly at the others.

Jay responded, "Dr. Lodge, Um, Graham was, Um….. murdered on our second day at the island."

There was a cold silence for some time. Dr. Lodge couldn't believe his ears. He staggered towards the cushy sofa. He dropped down. Graham's Mom broke down almost immediately.

Dr. Lodge said, "All my fault….This is all my fault. I sent him on a trip and he died?"

Bella and Jones said together, "Wait what?"

Mr. Throne asked angrily, "Why didn't you inform us?"

Betty cried, "Mr. Throne, there was a huge storm. All networks and communication systems were blocked. And we didn't want to drag you down with us to this mess. We are sorry. We are so very sorry."

Bella asked, "Mr. Lodge, are you MANONYMOUS?"

Mr. Lodge explained, "Holden Goldson and I are friends. Of course Graham didn't know that. Also, he didn't know that Goldson was his company head."

Bella interrupted, "But he is the one who told us that you paid for him to get a higher paying job there."

Lodge wept, "Miss Throne, he never knew that Goldson was his boss. Goldson is a businessman, it is true, but he had rivals in his other side businesses, leaving out the Manor. So it was important that Goldson used another name in his other businesses. Holden Sowerberry."

"Only this name was known to Graham, who had never met Goldson before in his life. Goldson had some plans for another business. For crushing our rivals. And Holden suggested that Graham shouldn't know about this, because he was going to join his company, and also because one of our rivals is a shareholder there. He wasn't supposed to know that we were going to crush his empire. So we didn't want to take a risk of involving Graham in this. Holden said that we could send Graham on a trip to his Manor, meanwhile we complete scheming against our rivals. The graduation trip was just a cover. But it would have looked shady if we sent Graham alone for a graduation trip. So, we sent you a mail, inviting his six best buddies. Holden suggested the name MANONYMOUS too. I'm going to cut all business with him now. I will just practice in my hospital from now on. I will never indulge in business. It cost me my Graham."

Just then, when everyone was about to cry, a car approached. And the couple that stepped out of the 1961 Chevrolet Impala convertible, were the other two unexpected guests, after Jones. Ansy and Jake Umnom.

Jones sighed, "Good God!"

Both of them looked really aristocratic. They were one of the richest business people in town. And were blood relatives to the Thrones.

Ansy said, "Celia told me that you kids were coming today. We wanted to surprise you by showing up like this. But honestly, I am most surprised. Why is Johan here?"

Jones smiled, "Hey Sis, I haven't talked to you since I left for Alaska except for getting the boat. I'm sorry about that. It must've come as a surprise because-"

Mrs. Throne interrupted, "Ansy, these kids were in danger. Grave danger. Their friend, Dr. Lodge's son....died, while they were on their graduation trip. And they had the audacity not to call us. And look who they contacted instead! A man who tarnished our family name. My name."

"Oh dear! Celia I'm guessing it's because of the storm. I heard that one had approached the Cormawall islands. They might not have had the means to call and inform you. That's why they asked Johan, who called me to rent a boat. Right Bella?"

"Exactly! See Ma, Auntie Ansy understands."

Jones cut in, "Can't we all leave our past behind just this time? A kid is dead! We have to stay together. No one's leaving the house. As far as I know, the killer might already be here. In town."

Jake Umnom said, "Ansy, I told you it was a bad idea coming here. Now we are all trapped in the midst of murder investigation, while our business is left back at home."

While the others looked terrified, Mrs. Throne spoke angrily, "Why Johan, blame this on me again won't you!"

Bella shouted, "Mom! Cut it out! Can we discuss this family feud later? After we get the target off our backs?"

The others nodded in agreement.

Chapter 8

A Discreet Analogy and An Unusual Hunch

'You reap what you sow', is a very popular saying. But it does not hold good in certain cases. Did Graham actually deserve cold-blooded murder? Had The Artist actually returned? Was someone among them lying about something? To protect someone? Someone like a dangerous ally?

In a way, the Throne residence was the archetype of a classy haunted house.

Exactly like the Horror Manor. Owned by business tycoons. The similar atmosphere of pin drop silence. Lucky's howl. And a potential murderer?

They were all at the dinner table. Looking down, peering deep into their plates. As if they seek answers from their own reflections projected by the crystal. Jones spoke up, "No one leaves the house until we track that madman down."

Mr. Umnom sulked, "Say what now? You might be jobless, but my wife and I have business to attend to. We are leaving at dawn tomorrow."

Jones made quick changes to his tone. "Would you like a killer, who specifically hunts down business people, to come with you in that fancy little car of yours?"

Ansy said, "Johan, is it, The Artist? That's impossible."

Jones replied, "I'm afraid so, Ansy."

Ansy sighed, "Then I guess we're staying."

Mr. Umnom agreed as he continued to sulk.

The night was calm. But no one could sleep. The Throne Residence was extremely crowded. Eight rooms it had, but the seven pairs of parents took those luxurious rooms. Jones slept in the guest room and the six young-adults crashed in the sofas, in the den. Those were the primary reasons, but to add to that, they were supposed to stay there until their killer was found. Who would be able to sleep? Bella twisted and turned to be liberated from the thoughts of murder. But she couldn't sleep. She patted her blonde head, and sat up. She asked herself, "Have I missed something? Something crucial? Yes! That's it! However could Uncle Jones be sure that it was The Artist? He was a serial killer. He would never break his chain by killing Graham. It had to be someone else. But still there is some ambiguity left. Claudius McKinsley. It was obvious that his murderer was The Artist. There was all the necessary evidence to support that. Could there be two murderers? I have to confront Uncle Jones."

She waited for the sun to rise. And finally, it was morning. Birds never chirped at their residence. Let alone chirping, birds never even came around there. Probably because of that grave atmosphere. Bella ran up the three-storeyed building, until she reached the guest room.

She found that her Uncle was shifting from channel to channel in a hurried manner. Every channel's breaking news was 'Son of Dr. Lodge murdered in newly renovated Horror Manor. Owner Goldson taking a vow of silence.'

Bella said, "Morning!"

Jones wished her back.

"So, what does it say in the news? That Goldson killed him?"

Jones replied, "No. Goldson has an alibi. He was in Hawaii. In fact, he is still in Hawaii. So, it's not him."

"Uncle, I wanted to talk to you about something."

"Oh, I know dear. You want to know why I was sure that the Artist had murdered Graham. I was actually expecting this query. You see, we don't know who to trust. Okay? Who knows, someone in this very house might be our person. I was just keeping ideas open. We might've missed the canvas in both Louis' and Graham's cases. It is a probability."

Although she didn't get a proper answer, Bella nodded.

"I just thought this up last night, but isn't there a chance that there were no canvases in the first place? Couldn't we have two killers on the loose?"

"I am not denying it."

Bella spoke again, "And also, since our killer or killers are very crooked, would MANONYMOUS actually be a name? It's not even a real word. Can't it be a hoax?"

"We can never know, Bella. I shared the name with my old friends in service, and they used a computer code to find out the actual word from the anagram. But as far as we know, if this is a proper noun, there can be a hundred thousand possibilities."

Just then, Celia walked up to their room.

"Breakfast's ready. Come down, Bella."

Bella looked at Jones, feeling sorry that her mother didn't call him.

He said, "Oh don't bother. I'll come anyway. Her anger will come to rest when I crack this case and give you all peace."

And quite abruptly, Bella said, "Uncle, please come and live with us."

He smiled.

"No dear. The rest of the family wouldn't want that. I'm just happy you offered."

After breakfast, Jay asked Jones, "So, what should we do?"

"We won't do anything. You will leave this alone. All of you. And stay here. I will take the case."

Bella was disappointed, "But Uncle, we want to help."

Celia said, "Of course not! None of you steps out of this house. You all are going to stay here with your parents until he finds the killer."

Jones spoke, "Bella, your Mum is right. This is not some fairy tale. This is murder, and possibly serial murder. I don't want you kids, the targets, in the middle of this. You must stay safe. Right here in this house, where we hope that MANONYMOUS or whoever that is, won't harm you."

Jones said, "I'm just going to run to the police station. They gave me a call. They hinted that it's important that I come."

Bella said, "Brief us on what the cops say when you get back."

They anxiously waited. They were sitting in the living room, binging The Big Bang Theory. Just then, they heard a noise. The noise of a huge glass breaking. Betty gasped, "Guys, did you hear that?"

And then there was a scream. It was Mr Lodge. They ran up.

They saw Mr Lodge on the ground. And a shattered chandelier.

Graham's Mom cried, "The chandelier just dropped down. I don't know why. If he hadn't gotten up from that chair, he would have…."

"Oh my God!" said Bella. "Someone deliberately did that?"

An hour later, Jones returned from the station, looking as if he ate raw fish.

Bella went up to him and questioned, "Well, what did they say?"

All of them looked at him eagerly.

Jones sighed, "Goldson…. He died in Hawaii. He was poisoned."

After they heard the news, it took some time to settle down. The sun began to settle down too. Bella was thinking so much that she almost bit off her nails. She couldn't stop herself from asking Jones what must have happened. "Uncle, what do you think happened? Had our killer sent an assassin, or did the killer personally go there?"

"The latter is impossible, so we can rule that out. My best guess is an assassin. Or he or she might have a helper, who runs errands for him or her."

Betty chimed in, "Hmm. So the chandelier was just a coincidence?"

Jones said, "That's what I meant. I looked around, and the chandelier was definitely cut from the top. That's why I said that there might be two people. One here, and one in Hawaii. Someone in this house is making us look like fools."

"Uncle, can we please help. Since now there is a possibility of two criminals, can we do something? Anything?"

Jones sighed. "Ah, yes. You may search about the house, and find out who is responsible for the chandelier mishap. The cops and I will take care of Hawaii and Goldson. Are we clear?"

All nodded.

Chapter 9

The Riddles of Death

The road to hell is always paved with good intentions. That is quite true, but what would happen if it was the other way round. The road to heaven can be painful. Treacherous. And paved with the losses of loved ones. There was absolutely no doubt where Bella and her friends' road was leading. Straight to hell. But the only different aspect was that their road was paved with deadliness. It could have been anticipated easily. It was not like they were spinning some flax-golden tale anyway. But the only important thing was, whether they would make it alive, after what was coming for them. Something ominous indeed.

The next morning, Bella and her friends started weaving their murder board. Or more precisely, two murder boards. One for MANONYMOUS, and one for The Artist. But they had no dots to join. No lines to connect. All they had was a couple of names. Totally unrelated. Although they had no clue or lead, deep down, they knew that they had to find out who was hunting them down, and who caused the irrevocable death of their friend, and who would be the cause of their deaths too.

They sat down in the living room. Thinking about what they must do next. Who would have conspired and planned to kill Mr. Lodge. Bella sighed. Losing hope little by little. Just when all of them received a notification. Together. They scrolled through their texts. And what they found was a complete game changer. A message. From none other than MANONYMOUS. They stared at it in horror.

And what they saw was,

Hello dears (who are soon to be visiting the cemetery),

I am so glad you are home. Finally, I can catch my breath. You are all with me now. Solve my little riddle, and save your dear souls.

"I know you

Will think of

Murder, your friend

Bella's final wish.

Mother, save me!"

Rat about this to your joke of a detective Jones and I will end him.

With heaps of blood and bones,

M.

Jay said, switching his phone off, "What in God's name is this thing?"

Betty chimed in, "Great. Now he's stalking us?"

Bella gasped, "Wait! There is an attachment. A video. Oh my god! It's Mr. Lodge. A video of the chandelier falling!

Why would he take a video of that? We have to tell Uncle."

Jane said, "No. The message said that we shouldn't. Or else he will…."

Bella read the message again. She suddenly realized something. "Guys, what do we reckon from this message?"

Georgie and Betty started chiming in with observations.

"It's obviously from MANONYMOUS. He is stalking us. Blackmailing us."

Bella shook her head, "Y'all are missing something. Something crucial. Is this the way we normally send messages? Don't you think it's written in a little old-fashioned way? It's texting. We usually use short-forms. Like 'u' for 'you'. This person has written it in a cliched serial-killerish way. Don't you think?"

Charlie said, "She is right. But in my opinion, we shouldn't read too much into this. Maybe the killer is just mocking us, for all we know. And since we all got this threat, can we partially rule out the possibility of this stalker being one of us? We were together when the chandelier fell anyway. So, we can actually be sure that none of us is a rat. And besides, we can't even track this text. I tried just now. I think it was sent from a burner."

"So it is someone in the house? Our parents are suspects?"

"We can rule out Dr. Lodge. He was a victim. And his son just died. And Goldson planned all this. Or someone made him plan all this," Bella said, "And also, this riddle is our main priority. By the way, I guess we have all day to solve this."

Just then, she heard a sound. "Kling!" It was her phone. Another message from MANONYMOUS. It said, "You have 2 hours!"

She said, "Someone is watching us. Is spying on us. There must be a camera somewhere here."

Jay interrupted her, "Bella, but what if this is a ploy? I mean, just a way for him or her to make sure that we will listen and that we are scared?"

Jay got a notification at that very moment. "Don't test me. I already know that you are scared of me. Ah, just to prove your theory wrong, tea-time is in two hours!"

"Ughh! Now what does that mean?"

Bella said, "It means that we should not waste a minute. And don't, at any cost, tell Uncle."

They started working. But they couldn't find anything. They were absolutely clueless. It was an ambiguous message. What was supposed to be understood from it?

An hour passed by, like the zephyr.

Bella said, "Guys, anything?"

"No, not yet. But you know why I can't concentrate? It's because Jay is texting someone in upper case, which annoys me," said Betty.

Jay shouted, "Live with it! Not my problem that your OCD doesn't fancy me texting in upper case."

Betty gasped, "Oh my God, that's it! Bells, take that text again."

Hello dears (who are soon to be visiting the cemetery),

I am so glad you are home. Finally I can catch my breath. You are all with me now. Solve my little riddle, and save your dear souls.

"I know you

Will think of

Murder, your friend

Bella's final wish.

Mother, save me!"

Rat about this to your joke of a detective Jones and I will end him.

With heaps of blood and bones,

M.

"Check out the lines in quotes. Now look at the words beginning in caps, and read them in one sentence."

The others eagerly gaped.

"I will murder Bella's mother."

Bella gasped, "What in the world? Guys, I think I know how he is going to try and kill her. Come on!"

They ran down to the tea garden. The parents were drinking tea. Bella rushed to her mother, and pushed her down.

Celia screamed, "Good Lord!"

The cup of tea spilled on the lawn. Bella was relieved.

Mr. Throne shouted, "What do you think you are doing, Bella?"

"There was....there was poison in Ma's tea," Bella wheezed.

"That's it! We wish to get out of here, with our lives," said the other parents.

They looked at each other as if they had seen a ghost.

Just that moment, Jones rushed into the garden.

"What in God's name is going on here?"

Dr. Lodge gasped, "Someone tried to poison Celia."

Jones said, "Kids, come with me."

He took the six to his guest room.

He asked, "Are you kids hiding something from me? I know you are, because you all looked relieved when the tea was spilled. I saw you when I was getting out of the car. But when you saw me, your demeanour inclined towards nervousness. Tell me what's going on right now!"

Bella never liked lying to her Uncle. She never had to. He could always see right through her.

"Uncle, we were sitting in our room, working on our murder board. I went downstairs for some High Point. Holly had kept the tea to heat up. She wasn't there to supervise, and I saw a bottle of rat poison in the dustbin. So, I deduced that someone had put it in Ma's tea while Holly was away."

Jones interrogated, "But how did you know that the poison was in her tea? Couldn't it have been in anyone else's?"

Bella mumbled, "That, um, Ma drinks only rose tea. When I checked, it wasn't light pink. The colour had changed. So....."

Jones said, "Okay. That was a smart move. Good work Bella! Now get some dinner and go to bed. I know that you guys haven't been able to sleep properly for the past few days. Take a break for today."

They smiled in acknowledgement, and returned to the living room. Just as they reached the living room, away from Jones, Bella got a new text. The others were tired, asleep. So, she kept it to herself.

It said,

Hello Bella,

Well played. What doesn't kill you, makes you stronger I guess. But I doubt that you will be able to match my calibre in the next round of this Grand Hunt.

M.

She texted back.

Just understand this, you sicko! You will never be able to hurt us. Ever again!

Just that second, a text was returned,

Are you sure? How many people do you think I have murdered, mutilated, etcetera. I have an enormous amount of experience. But you will too. Soon. You, your friends, and your family, will sweat blood.

M.

Chapter 10

A Luke-Cold Revelation:

Dead men tell no tales. At least, that's what is assumed by most. But actually, when we think about it, dead men tell more tales than alive ones. Bella's mind had become a butcher's shop at that point. New thoughts came like new animals. Nevertheless, in each of her ideas, schemes, hunches, they were chopped up like poor little lambs. After the last text she received from MANONYMOUS, something was still stuck in her mind. MANONYMOUS had said that he or she had a lot of experience. Does that mean……. That MANONYMOUS is in fact……The Artist?

Although it was a good assumption, Bella decided to keep her hunch quiet. What if it was wrong? The last thing she wanted was to drag everyone into another downward spiral.

Another thought came to her mind. What was he implying when he was talking about her going to be experienced too? Did that mean that she had to kill people?

On the other side of the house was Jones. No other case has ever made him spiral like this. Did he have a few hunches of his own? Were they similar to Bella's?

He said, "I bet a thousand times that something is going on with the children. Why has The Artist returned? How will I ever tell Bella why this is happening? That it's all because of me….."

He was interrupted. "Hey Jones! When can we get back? By tomorrow at least?" questioned Jake.

"What part of 'everyone here is in danger', do you not understand? Hell, even you could be a murderer. A serial killer."

Jake looked nervous. "Jones, why would you even think that I am responsible for The Artist's work? You think I have the nerve to chop people up like that?"

Jones gasped, "Who told you that? No one here ever mentioned the M.O of The Artist. How could you possibly know?"

"Well, uhh, Ansy told me... of course. I was curious about what you people were discussing the night we came."

Jones was still not satisfied. He never knew Jake to be a curious soul, thirsty for knowledge. But he left it there. It could be anyone. Even Celia. When the thought of Celia came to his mind, he realised something. If he was right, then Bella was in grave danger. He then understood the need to tell her everything. What exactly happened 17 years ago…..

He went to the living room. Bella was there. Thinking. He started up the conversation.

"Good morning dear! How is the weather?"

Bella noticed that something was wrong.

"Okay Uncle, spill it. You're clearly trying to start a difficult conversation. It's okay. You can tell me anything at this point. Because even you or I could be a cold-blooded murderer."

"Okay Bella. I have to tell you this. It's now or never.

I didn't tell you the whole story, about what happened 17 years ago. I said that I only suspected your mother to be The Artist. And that's because I hadn't the slightest idea that it was so much worse than I had imagined. I told you about the canvases which were evidently Celia's. But there was more than that. I saw her, Bella. I saw her walking away from Mr. McKinsley's dead body. Who I think, might be the father of Claudius McKinsley. I knew he sounded familiar. I never told you, because I knew that if I were to tell you that, then I would have had to tell you this too. I said that I suspected her, because I saw it with my own eyes. She was walking away from the garage where we found his body. I didn't report it because I didn't have solid proof, as I didn't see her face. I knew it was her, because I saw her finishing up her painting from behind and leaving it there. She was a red-head too. It couldn't have been anyone else. Because all of us had solid alibis except for her. So, I walked back to the house. And I asked her why she did what she did. She behaved as if she knew nothing. She got extremely angry, and told Mom. Everyone was disappointed with me. After a while, I realized that it really could have been anyone who wanted to frame Celia. I have tried to follow up on this case since then. But I got no new leads. Celia has always been an innocent person. And I know it. I've always loved her. But if it is her, then a part of her mind which is uncontrollable, has been doing all this."

Bella looked shocked. "Uncle, are you telling me that my mother is a prime suspect in this long-term killing spree?"

"Oh dear, I'm sorry, but the truth might always seem bitter."

"No, Uncle. Why should you apologize? It is only the potential truth. You should never have been disregarded because of this."

"Bella, you are one of the most rational people I have ever known, you know? You remind me of myself, back in the day. You must have real guts to accept something as horrifying as that."

Bella smiled, "I learnt that from you, Uncle. Now, my mother or not, I want to find who is doing these monstrous deeds. I have to."

The second half of the day, Bella spent her time staring at her murder board. But as usual, no new leads could be found. She didn't give up. She felt empty and bad that all this was happening to her and her friends just because of some madman who was jobless enough to go after people and also because of the fact that her friends were caught in this loop all because of her. Just then, she received a text from her worst nightmare. MANONYMOUS again. Her friends came running to her. She told them what Jones had told her. The text said:

Hello dears,

I'm so sorry for not spending enough time with you today. Well, I was busy preparing your next death hunt. Well, this one is going to be tough. Because it's your lives that are in the line! You kids, being responsible for your own death. Such craft! Here, each one has to make a choice. This is not ending so soon. Believe me when I say, this is no mere code-cracking.

You six dear children, Detective Jones is useless. You are going to be on your own. You have 2 hours for this short and sweet game. You kids must kill one among you. It can be anyone but Bella. This is mainly for her. She can't be killed off right now, can she? So, choose a person among you, and follow my teaching. Canvases are on my bed. Go find them. They might be a little dusty. But you'll get a lot of dirt and blood on them anyway, children. This is only part of the grandiose payback. That's all you'll get. Now run along! Start picking. I would recommend killing off saint Betty or that doofus Georgie. Now aren't they annoying! And oh, I almost forgot! Failure to deliver my orders will result in immediate termination of the whole clan. Believe me when I say that, I can burn the house and just kill everyone in it. And I bear no ill-will to dying. Anyway, killing everyone will fulfil my ambition in turn.

M.

They couldn't breathe. Bella then understood that was exactly what MANONYMOUS meant by experience. They sat in silence for minutes. They couldn't bring themselves to say anything. Georgie got up.

"Guys just kill me. I'm sick of living like this, under the spell of some tyrant. I just don't care anymore."

The others attempted to comfort him, while Bella suddenly had a thought.

"Guys, it's not Ma."

The others stared in shock. What did she mean? How was she so sure? Those were their thoughts.

"Okay see, MANONYMOUS is playing these mind games with us, to mess with us, and to derail us from finding something out. So, if it was my mother, and if we are suspecting her, then why would she say that the canvases are on her own bed? That's where MANONYMOUS went wrong. Only a person trying to frame her would say such a thing. So rule out Ma and Dr. Lodge. I'm sure. And I'm happy that Uncle might be right. Someone probably hired a red-head look-alike of Ma to frame her. But I can't tell him just yet."

Betty reminded, "But now we are left with nothing. It could be anyone else. Literally anyone."

Bella replied. "No. We know one thing. Someone who detests my mother is doing all this. For 17 years. But again that could be anyone. Our parents knew each other way before we were even born. So, we're back to square one."

Jay chimed in, "But Bella, did they all have access to your mother's canvases? I don't think so."

Jane sighed, "All of them were really close friends. I'm sure that they did have that privilege."

Elizebeth, who spent most of her time thinking and observing passively, shared her thoughts after a long time.

"Jane's right. We have only ruled out two people. Now, we are sure that one of our parents is, and always has been, MANONYMOUS."

Chapter 11

Poor Little Miscreants and a 'Sweet' Suspicion:

Mistrust and suspicion trigger people to do so many things. Making them miscreants. They are forced to do something unlawful themselves. Due to the external suppression and control of some kind of entity. The residents of the manor could relate to this a lot. After all, they were mere puppets in the grand show of the ingenious MANONYMOUS. He seemed almost impossible to stop. But there was someone. Someone unimportant, that they were missing out. Now did they have something to do with this? With everything? For 17 whole years?

They were in a serious crisis. They were literally just asked to take the life of one of their friends. How could they possibly do that? How would they ever live with that sin later on? They had to think. There is always a silver lining to everything.

Bella's mind was running wild. So many thoughts to process. She found no way out. She took out her phone, and texted MANONYMOUS.

"Stop this now. Please.

Is there any other way out? Please! Why are you doing this to us?"

She got a reply within seconds.

"Bella……Bella…….Bella…….

The only way out is to just finish off one person. All of you are stains on the world anyway. Just do it.

Darn! Now look what you've done? You made me feel pity for you.

Fine…..Just kill your mother then. She is one of the reasons why everything happened. Why! Everyone's lives are interconnected in a single spiral of death. Now don't tell me that you can't kill her either.

Fine…..I'll give you the whole day. Enough? Then you'll get more than enough time to wipe those pathetic tears off of your pretty little face.

I'm busy. Bye now!"

M

Bella gasped.

"Oh my God! I have a lead! Guys, think! Who is the one person who has access to this house all the time, and has known my mother for more than 17 years?"

Jane stuttered, "Uh, your Dad?"

"Jane, don't be stupid. It has to be Holly!"

"Bella, are you seriously accusing your house-help? Doesn't she have anything better to do around here, rather than running around and killing people?"

Bella was reluctant to concur. "Look. The pieces fit perfectly. She has been around long enough to know exactly where to set cameras. I know that she could lip-read. In fact, she's the one that taught me the art. That's how she knew what exactly we were talking about."

The others shook their heads in disapproval.

Betty asked, "Bella, then how do you explain the painting canvases with blood? The killer has to be a skilled artist. And the only skilled artist I know is your Mom, but she's not our person."

Bella replied, "Guess who taught my mother art? Don't underestimate Holly. She's extremely intelligent and talented."

Jay found it hard to believe. "But Bella, she's so sweet. She always makes us cream croissants and fruit cake and is too innocent to be a killer. And that too for more than 17 years. It's almost impossible."

Bella sighed, "Uncle Jones always says that a crafty killer knows how to masquerade his or her way through life."

Jay asked, "So we just go ahead and tell Jones, and get her arrested before she makes us murder Bella's Mom?"

Charlie shook his head. "Don't be an utter idiot, Jay. First, we must find tangible proof that clearly points to Holly. Then we proceed."

They thought of breaking into her room and looking for any kind of evidence, text trail, poison, knives, anything. And so, they did. They knew the time when Holly stepped out for her evening errands and her visit to the store for supplies. They searched for about an hour. Desperately.

They thought they couldn't find anything. Bella said, "Well, this doesn't look promising. Unless…"

The others made gestures indicating curiosity.

"Well, we need to know what we're looking for. And what motive does Holly have, to try to frame Mom?"

Betty chimed in. "Well, we know it's not money. She is indeed intelligent. She would know better ways to plan a heist, in lieu of executing carefully planned serial murders. So, my best idea is a personal vendetta against Celia."

Bella intervened, "Absolutely not. Holly loves my Mom. She has always cared for her. Maybe, just maybe, we're missing something. Wait, the portraits! Oh my God! I remember now. That's what the argument was about! Yes! So guys, way back, like about 15 years back, something happened. Alright this may sound silly, but Holly dwells in emotion. So, this counts. Auntie Ansy told me this some years back. As you guys know, Ma has always loved art. And there was this huge family occasion, where portraits of every person in the family, family members, house-helps, secretaries, literally everyone were painted. And Ma, being the painter in the family, was the one who had to paint that time. Family tradition. And she didn't paint Holly's portrait. All of them asked her why, but she never really explained herself. The others left it, but Holly didn't. Ma has neither apologized, nor explained the reason for her being cross to Holly."

Jay commented, "But, Belles, this seems a little too puerile. That's the reason for a serial killer to murder for more than 17 years? Seems too trivial."

Bella sighed, "You guys didn't let me finish. Then a few years after that incident, she told me that Ma saw Holly talking to a bunch of her colleagues. Businessmen. When she asked her about it, what she said was, 'You were the one who pushed me away.' "

Jay said, "I guess that's enough for us to question her."

Some time later, when Holly returned from the supply store, they cornered her.

"Are you keeping something from us? Is that really why you hate Celia now? Are you behind all of this? 17 years? Are you The Artist?" – Those were the questions that were confusing Holly at that moment.

Holly took a deep breath. "My dears, why are you asking me all this? I don't understand."

"Then tell us what you were doing with those businessmen? Years back... And when Bella's Mom asked you about it, you said something that puts you in a shady position now."

Holly didn't spill the beans yet. "Dears, I really don't know what you are talking about. I said all that out of anger."

"Wow if someone doesn't draw a picture of you, you get pissed? This is new."

"No no, you've got it all wrong. I wasn't angry about the drawing. I barely even remember whatever that was about. And I don't know why Celia started treating me badly. But I didn't care. I still loved her. I said all that to her because...."

Bella chimed in. "Tell us Holly, who are you protecting? Who are you covering for? Ma? Are you trying to be the antagonist here, making us think it was you?"

Holly shuddered. She snapped, "I said I did not send you those messages!"

Jay said, "Holly, we never mentioned messages. What are you getting at? You knew about that too didn't you?"

Holly trembled. Her lips twitched in fear. "Oh dear, what have I done! I-I should go. Excuse me."

Bella shouted, "You can't leave! It is Ma isn't it... You knew what we were up to. You probably kept tabs on us. And you knew it was Ma all along. You were protecting her. For 17 years. Even now….. You pretended to hate her, so that we would deduce that she was framed. And you sent that message, saying that canvases are on Ma's bed, you knew that we would rule her out because it reveals that someone was trying to frame her. And that we'd go after that person. You were ready to pose as a killer for her. Am I not right?"

Charlie said, "Bells, keep Holly here. We have to find Jones at once. Where the hell did he go anyway?"

Chapter 12

The Last Kill

Love makes a person do unspeakable, horrendous things. This love can be for friends, family, and most importantly, for oneself. There has been an age-long conflict within each and every person, about who one loves most. Another person, or themselves? That question remains unanswered. Well, at least till date. But the important thing here is, who does Holly love more? Herself, Celia, or was there someone else? Has she done all this for someone else? Or was she the original mastermind? Can anything be said at all?

'The oldest and strongest emotion of mankind is fear, and the oldest and strongest kind of fear is fear of the unknown.'

This very popular adage speaks volumes about people. People who have journeyed through the shallow waters of crime and murder with ease, saved their allies, and also, the people, sailing in ships driven by innocence, who have been drowned by the pirates, mentioned earlier. So, the only questions that remained, in the minds of Holly and the six sleuthing investigators, could be related. What went through the gang's minds was, why she was protecting

Bella's mother, and what motive she had, to slaughter the children of the people for whom she works. And more importantly, what Holly was thinking, was probably, or rather surely, whether she had rescued the right person from drowning and whether she has been trying to drown the wrong people all this time.

Another beautiful day. Jones could be seen, strutting the veranda. Contemplating the lake outside. He stared right through the ocean-blue water. Into his reflection. Bella approached him.

"Uncle, we are almost sure that it is Holly, but we still fail to understand why she would protect Ma."

Jones laughed. "How are you so sure it's your mother, Bella?"

"But Uncle, you're the one who gave us a hint that it might be Ma...Why are you doubting now?"

"Because, Bella, everything we see, looks the way we want it to look. Things that are perceived that way, may even be completely wrong. But be sure that Holly has a hand in whatever that has happened, and what is happening."

Bella said, "Can we please question her? I'm not supposed to be coming to you right now, but I think, since we have our criminal, it is safe to ask you to help us. So, can you come with us?"

Jones sighed, "Very well."

Back in the other side of the house, it was almost as if Holly was being held captive by Bella's friends. She trembled with fear. Not knowing how much longer she could keep all those secrets within her. She knew how intelligent Jones was and how he could easily extract all that she knew about MANONYMOUS from her. When she saw Jones, she tried playing the sympathy card.

"Johan, please tell me why I'm being held here. Do you suspect me? I've known you your whole life, Johan. You know me."

Johan replied, "Well, Holly, if Bella suspects you, I know that there's a reason. The only thing I was wondering about, was why Bella didn't come to me with this earlier. I suppose you have a hand in that too? Or were you just in on the serial killings that have been happening for the past 17 years?"

And that's when Holly realised that lying wasn't going to help her. She didn't know what to say. But she still had to protect whoever she was protecting. "You have no proof."

Jones added, "Well actually Holly, we don't require any kind of proof to consider you a suspect. Technically everyone here is a suspect. Unless the kids have any kind of threats or proofs making you, or anyone, for that matter, the prime suspect. So, Bella, do you have any kind of proof?"

Bella obviously didn't want to take an unnecessary risk. What they deduced from the texts was the same thing that Jones knew. That it had to be Holly. So why should she give extra unnecessary details, when it is possible that it could hurt Jones, like MANONYMOUS said?

"No Uncle. Nothing of the sort," Bella lied.

"Well then!" Jones believed her.

Holly said, "Know this Johan, I would never do anything to hurt these kids, or you, or anyone in this family. I have only protected you. Always. Or....at least tried to. I....I must go now. Excuse me."

They didn't stop her that time, even though vestiges of doubt remained in their minds. But they decided to give her the benefit of the doubt. Afterall, she was like family.

It began to rain a while after that. The fulfilling smell of petrichor had infected the air over the Throne residence. It was almost ironic, because, as it started showering outside the house, the sound of the rain had almost masked and silenced the voices of restless minds, souls, and moreover, it brought about tranquility. But what was about to happen next, was expected, as well as unexpected.

Everyone was downstairs. Except for Holly. She was cleaning out a room. No one could hear her from downstairs. That was when Mr. Umnom created a fuss.

"Where is my tea? I kept it somewhere over here, and I went to attend a business call. Did the kids take it? Ansy, was that you? Jones?"

Ansy sulked, "For the love of God, Jake! Just go ask Holly to get you another cup of tea. Why would any of us take your tea? We have other things to worry about. Don't be a child."

He continued being fussy. The others understood that there was no point in preaching. So, everyone tried to ignore him. A while after that, Bella sensed that something was wrong. She asked, "Wait, where's Holly?"

Everyone looked just as surprised as she did. They ran upstairs, only to find Holly.....not dead. But petrified. She couldn't move. She had been screaming and shouting for a long time. But no one could hear her. Celia went up to her and asked, "Holly, what's wrong?"

Holly instantly moved backwards in fear. She was somehow afraid. Afraid, even of Celia's breath.

After much thought and discussion about what might've happened to Holly, Holly herself resolved the matter, by telling them that it was just a traumatic childhood memory that was rekindled by her mind when she thought about something. But Bella didn't buy it.

She inquired, "Uhh Holly, you're telling us, that you just happened to remember a childhood memory suddenly? Has this ever happened before? Or did you see something? Or someone, maybe?"

The look on Holly's face changed. She clenched her fists in fear and nervousness.

"Nothing of the sort, dear. I just remembered something....It's all in the past...Never you mind dear. I'm sorry to have troubled all of you. Excuse me."

Jones smiled, "Don't worry about it, Holly. It happens. A cold memory that is rekindled in the mind, is destined to take a toll on one's mental state."

Everyone seemed surprised, except for Bella, and the others who knew.

Some time later, Bella and her friends got a text.

Hello dears,

Honestly....It has been so long! But you know why I'm talking to you right now.....Everything that has been happening is ultimately the result of your actions. Today you have really angered me. This was supposed to be my last kill. Everything would've ended. But yet again, you had to ruin everything. As I said, in the end of it all…..you will pay….all of you. Until then…….count your days.

M.

Jay sulked, "Not this again….. Bella, can we please, please tell your Uncle?"

Bella didn't concur. She didn't want anything bad to happen to him, because clearly, the psychopath they were dealing with was dangerous. But the question is, how far would he or she go to complete the so-called quest? And also, if the killer was in the house, and their victim was right under their nose, then why was the killer only threatening to kill them, when they had a lot of time to actually do it? What was MANONYMOUS' actual aim? When would it finally end?

In the mean time, Holly thought about what Jones had said to console her. About her 'cold memory'. She could understand that it was not a consolation. It was a sheer threat. That he was going to keep tabs on her. That he knew what Holly hadn't told a soul. That she was a suspect. She feared if Jones had found out about what actually happened upstairs. Did he actually know who was terrorizing her? She hoped not. Because if he did, everything would go down in the seventeen-year old treacherous swamps of Jones' investigation. They would be able to deduce the rest easily if they knew who it was. Or would they?

She heard footsteps. It was Jones. He walked over there, and stood beside her.

"I know, Holly. But don't worry, I won't tell."

Holly's eyes teared up, "Johan, that was a warning. I know that I'll be killed too. I am the only one who knows the whole story. The only one."

Jones tried persuading her to confess to everything. But she didn't budge.

"Johan, I will never confess to anything. If I do, that evil will come for you and Bella next. I know it. And you can never make me confess. You still have no proof. And I am praying that it will remain that way. Nobody can ever know."

Jones didn't lose hope. "Holly, you know that if we don't do something now, we are endangering the lives of many people here. I mean it. This can't be controlled. The killer has helpers too. When we talk about the killer, we should not use names. They might be listening in on us even now. But first, I must figure out why MANONYMOUS is so mad at me and the whole town, just because I made an accusation. And that too, seventeen years back. I apologized for it too. I doubt whether that's the only reason why MANONYMOUS has been harassing Bella and her friends. Their own...."

Bella interrupted him, "Uhh Uncle, Detective Davies just called for you. He wanted to meet with you at someplace called, Woodstew Lake? He said that you'd know what he meant."

Jones looked surprised. He said, "Thank you dear, I'll get to it immediately." He left abruptly, leaving Holly and Bella, oblivious.

Chapter 13

Oblivious? Maybe not

Something that frustrates most people, is the instance where their obliviousness becomes their own enemy, but turns out to be a boon for some others. It's almost like rain. You don't know when to expect it. The clouds might seem to cover up the skies for a while. But does it always rain? Maybe not. The clouds tend to be deceptive. Hiding the world from what something truly is. And if it rains, it might be bad for the bats. They can no longer detect the presence of the enemy. Lurking, waiting to ambush them from under the mask of wilderness. And those enemies welcome the rain with warm hands.

Although the above is true, it is certainly ironic. Just like how obliviousness makes someone insecure, it can spare them from apprehension. Sadness. Loss. Death. Knowing that someone knows that one knows nothing about something really isn't futile in some scenarios.

But considering the status quo of Throne Manor and its residents, both are not wrong. When one loses, the other gains. Or both suffer losses, or gain something or the other. Everything might just seem plausible.

The zephyr blew steadily near Woodstew Lake. The fresh water was blue, both literally and metaphorically. Two cold footsteps made Jones turn around.

"Ah Davies, I was expecting you. What do you have for me?"

"Good day, Jones. Remember a few weeks back I told you about the anagram? MANONYMOUS? Well, I thought that there were a million possibilities where a lot of them could have been plausible solutions to the anagram. I was rechecking our program and someone had tampered with it. Our lead technician can affirm it. Someone deliberately messed with it. To delay our investigation. Anyone in the house, who even remotely has access to a personal computer that shares a connection with your device could have done this. Whoever it was, did what he or she had to do very neatly. No traces whatsoever. Even our trained staff couldn't get anything on this genius. We're not being able to revive the program either. There's no way to redo this again. Do you have anything to say?"

Jones smiled, "Everything triggers something else. Maybe we aren't destined to receive this information now. Maybe it can trigger something bad. Maybe it's in our best interest. Speaking from personal experience, sometimes the truth finds you before you seek the truth yourself. You've just got to wait."

Davies looked utterly perplexed. "Umm so Jones, you don't want to recover the program?"

Jones replied, "No, Davies. I have another plan in mind. Retrieving the program will only meddle with my plan. All I need now is time."

"But at what cost? Someone else's death? I can't allow you to do that, Jones. I say we recover the program, find this psycho, and get on with what's left of our lives."

Jones interrupted, "Ok then tell me this. This whole time at the Manor, did MANONYMOUS murder anyone? No. Did we get any kind of death threats, or any kind of threats, for that matter? No. We don't have to rush anything. We have time. Trust me on this one. And yes, we may be able to find out who this person is from your program, but what do we do after that? He or she has possibly been keeping tabs on everyone in the house the whole time. Maybe we're being watched even now, who knows? If MANONYMOUS gets to know of us developing something like this, that would only trigger him or her to complete their quest faster and smarter. MANONYMOUS will be unstoppable. Invincible. Believe me, I've had my share of solved cases and psychological hypotheses, which are famously regarded even now. Don't take any kind of action without my consent. My family's welfare is at stake here."

Davies finally came around. "Alright, but if this becomes the cause for the culmination of their plans, it's all on you. You will be held accountable for the downfall of your family and for that deranged killer's resurrection."

As Jones walked back to his car, he was on the verge of having second thoughts. He suppressed all his thoughts and emotions. "Jones, you know very well that you are the only person who can save them. But you must hide these things for a few more days. For this town's sake."

A day passed. Bella had been staring at her phone for hours when the others told her to calm down.

Bella snapped at them. "The last text we got from him was to 'count our days.' "

Jay said, "Bella, you're really not worried about the threat, are you?"

"No, no. that's not what's been bothering me for some time now. It's just that.....Haven't you guys noticed something wrong about MANONYMOUS? He or she, has been threatening to kill someone or the other for a while now. But isn't doing so. Why do you think that is?"

Betty chimed in, "Like your Uncle has been suggesting, this is the same serial killer who has been plaguing the town for the past 17 years. Their modus operandi was different. There are no records or proof of him threatening anyone. And also, the people he or she killed in the past, were all allegedly corrupted. None of us can be sorted into that category. So maybe this time, that person is trying to get something done, or send a message, and not actually trying to kill us?"

The others nodded in agreement. Just then Jones hurriedly asked all of them to come down.

When they came downstairs they saw the breaking headlines. *Mysterious murder in Hawaii. Man stabbed to death. Police confirms the unidentified armed man to be an assailant of some sort.*

Bella looked shocked, "Uncle, you don't think...."

"Yes Bella....It can't be just a coincidence. I highly doubt it. Did anyone leave the house this week?"

Mr. Throne replied, "Yes. In fact, some of us did. The Lodges and our business team left for New York. I know,

Johan, you asked us not to leave, but our business depended on that deal. And it was a huge success."

"It's okay. Bella, come with me."

They went to the garden, and Jones explained, "Bella, this was MANONYMOUS's second last kill. He probably wanted to tie up all the loose ends, by killing Goldson's killer. Another one who knew the truth about his agenda. Holly was supposed to be the last one. But he failed. Which means, he will try again. So, please keep an eye on Holly at all times. She has much explaining to do at the end of everything." Immediately after saying this, Jones walked back to the mansion, leaving Bella perplexed. She had so many questions in her mind, blocking all the doors of her mind for her thoughts to escape. What did Uncle mean when he said, 'At the end of everything.'? Was he implying that he knows what's going to happen?

Bella returned to the house. She called her gang together, and told them, "Guys, I think Uncle Jones knows stuff that we don't. I mean, he keeps implying things indirectly, forcing me to infer. I mean, he's been doing this for a long time now, I think we should confront him. Thoughts?"

Betty remarked, "You know, you're right. He probably knows things. But do you think it's wise to find out more than we are supposed to know? Maybe he isn't telling us what he knows, because we might not want to hear it, or maybe because he's worried that it might get out of hand? I don't think we should confront him right away. Let's wait for him to tell us about his deductions."

Bella agreed, half-heartedly. Without telling the others, she sneaked out of the house that night, and took a bus to the police station. She had remembered something that her Uncle mentioned to her long back. There was a code to decipher the anagram, MANONYMOUS. Although he had told her that there were too many possibilities, Bella was almost prepared to even look at each and every one of them. She entered the station, and found Davies filling out some reports.

She asked, "Uhh Hi! Mr. Davies, I'm sorry for showing up here so late, but actually, Uncle Jones wanted to know about the results of the computer code that you had developed to crack the anagram. Can I have it to take to him?"

Davies looked confused. "Bella, dear, your Uncle told me that he didn't need it. I've known the man for a long time now, and something I do know about him is that he means what he says. He never has second thoughts on things, however urgent the situation may be. Now then, why would he send you now? And that too this late! We studied at the academy together, and I'm very sure that 2 a.m. is way past his bedtime."

Bella was searching for the perfect lie to tell an intelligent detective. "Actually, he had an epiphany! I know he is not a night owl, but he has been worrying about things lately, and he was probably up all night thinking about the next step."

"But what about the plan that he said he had?"

"Erm, he figured that it wouldn't work out. Please, he really wants help."

"Ok, but protocol wouldn't allow me to hand it to you. He is awake, isn't he? I'll come over with you right now, and I'll hand it over directly to him. How about that?"

Bella clenched her fists. She smiled and said, "Oh that's okay, Sir. He texted me right now, asking me to return, and that he'll collect it tomorrow. Bye now."

Before Detective Davies could utter even a single word, Bella fled the scene. She practically ran for her life, leaving Davies in utter confusion.

She stepped out of the station, and ran to the main road for a bus, sliding the printed results of the code into her back pocket, after stealthily stealing it away as she distracted Davies with questions and excuses. After she got home, she waited up till morning, and texted Davies that Jones won't be coming to collect the code, and is going through with his plan. She did this so that Davies wouldn't notice that the code had gone missing, thereby tying up the loose ends of her felony.

But to the misfortune of Bella, Davies arrived at the Throne residence, later that morning. Just as she saw him, she ran over there, and confronted him. "Good morning, sir! What are you doing here?"

"Well, good morning Bella. Since there was a lot of confusion last night and I think I misplaced a copy of the results, I thought I'd bring your Uncle a fresh copy of the results anyway. He can choose to use it or not, since he seemed unsure about it before."

"Oh! I'll go give it to him," said Bella, with half her heart cooling down, as he thought that he misplaced the original copy of the results.

"Oh no. I will directly hand it to him. I know he's here anyway, and besides, it seems that you kids can't be trusted with anything," he joked.

Bella didn't know what to say. She hadn't taken a look at the results yet. She didn't want Jones to see them either. Just then, Jones came out of the house.

"Oh Davies, did you bring the results with you? I thought I made it clear that I'll be going through with a plan of my own. Ah anyway, give it to Bella. She might be able to whip something up much faster."

Davies did as he was told, reminded Jones that he didn't have much time to execute his own plan, and took his leave. Bella finally let out a peaceful sigh of relief, as everything worked out in her favour. She had two things left to do. Firstly, she had to check out the results of the anagram code, and secondly, she had to spy on Jones and find out what his plan was, as it was clear to her that Jones wouldn't let her in on his plan otherwise.

Chapter 14

Viva The Pathos!

A feeling that everyone hates to experience is pity, from others. It lowers all barriers and shows you that you're not under the radar anymore. It puts you on the spot. Suddenly you become the centre of attraction, or at least, of fear. Everyone's gaze will be upon you, as if you're an outlander of some sort.

Pity is a feeling that one can never express in a kind way. Even though the emotion may be kind, its expression is always a pessimistic one. You can never tell someone that you feel sorry for them by trying to raise their spirits. It's basically a conveyance of sorrow as a worthless attempt to reduce sorrow. It never works. It only creates negativity in the minds of both parties. But expressing sorrow because of something, never occurred to MANONYMOUS. He or she had a different way of reacting to someone's misery. Happiness. Pure exultancy. For instance, doing good things for the subject of sorrow, like saving them from the burden of investigating someone, or more accurately, something. Sarcasm aside, it means destroying proof or evidence that is valuable or crucial to the subject of sorrow.

Nevertheless, every feeling lies. Every emotion is called out for bluffing at least once in a while, in the game of life. An emotion is a potentially lethal weapon that can be used to manipulate. That was MANONYMOUS's deal. Perpetual manipulation. Likewise, on the other side, Jones was quite capable of manipulation too. In his own way. But the difference was, his aim wasn't death. It was rejuvenation. To give a chance to a few people. To relive.

It was the next day. Night. Jones stood by the window of his room. He could see from there that Bella was perpetually staring at the results of the code. He could understand from the redness in her eyes and tiredness on her face, that she had been at it for aeons. It was a tiringly long list of more than a hundred thousand names. And that too, proper nouns. What was the guarantee that the culprit's name would be on it? Of course, the computer wouldn't have missed it. But there were way too many combinations. Although he previously said that Bella would be able to cover the whole list quickly, it was obviously a few days' work, if done manually. And also, her friends didn't know about all that. It had to be done manually, as no one knew what they were looking for. Jones didn't have the superpower of manoeuvring through that list either.

But it was exactly what Jones needed. Time. He needed to keep Bella busy. To keep her, and his 'plan' safe.

While all that happened, back in the other side of the house, Bella groaned. She told herself, "Now, 753 names left. Not so bad, huh?"

She told herself again, "753 more names....... I have to tell the gang. Why shouldn't they know? We've got amazing camaraderie going even with all this happening. I'll tell them about it. I have to."

Bella went to her friends to tell them what she'd been up to for the past few days. She explained everything to them. After she did, they expressed their wish to help her with it.

Jane asked, "Okay, I'm a little dubious here. How sure are you that the name of the killer is somewhere in this long list?"

Bella replied, "It's a long shot, but according to the program, it's supposed to be there."

The others said, "So we're basically looking for a needle in a haystack here."

Bella replied, "Well yeah, I know we're looking for a Hail Mary here but we at least have to try, you know? And also, we must find out what Uncle Jones is up to. I know he wouldn't tell us if we directly confront him. He's hiding something. I think he knows who's doing all this. Maybe that's why he didn't want the results of the code."

Jay asked, "You're saying that he's protecting someone? Us, or someone else?"

Bella didn't say anything. She had no idea herself. But they had to figure out a way to go about the conundrum.

The group started working. After a while, they were done. But they obviously weren't that lucky.

Bella said, "But how is this possible? I think there was an error in the code."

Betty shook her head. "Really, Bella? This was done by cops. In a police precinct. You think they wouldn't recheck their work?"

"You're right. Charlie, you know how to code this thing right? Recheck this program."

Charlie did as he was asked. He didn't need much time to give them an answer.

"Bella, there is an error. These are the results for a program to decipher the word 'synonymous'. Not MANONYMOUS. And when I try the same code for MANONYMOUS, it says 'no results'. Whoever changed the code probably did something to mess with that too."

"I think MANONYMOUS may have gotten into the precinct much before I did. He or she might've tampered with it when Davies wasn't around. I'm sure."

Jane suggested, "Well then, why don't we go up there and look at the footage?"

"Well Jane, the evil genius might have disabled the webcam systems. But no harm in going there to check it out."

They reached the station and immediately told Davies about the error in the code.

Davies looked confused. "Kids, I'll get you another copy of it after correcting it. Wait here."

He got into the system and tried to open the code. But it was bugged. All the data was deleted.

"Oh no! Who did this? The program took ages to make. And our technicians are not here either. I'm afraid your Uncle might've to go ahead with his plan."

Bella said anxiously, "Sir, can we please see the footage then? If that works anymore. We may be able to see who tampered with it then."

Davies and another officer checked if the webcam was enabled. And luckily, it was.

They called the gang over, and asked them to see if they recognized the person. It was a lady. But her face was covered by a hat. They could see her walking right into the precinct. And that's where the footage ended.

Bella said, "No doubt that it's Mom. Red hair, clothes, watch….."

Jay interrupted her. "Can't it be someone hired by MANONYMOUS? Another redhead? He or she was trying to frame your Mom. Everything fits."

"No. I'm sure it's Mom. Look at that tattoo on her right hand. I remember her having it years back. She got it when she took a trip to some kind of hill station for……painting. I don't think anyone could fake that perfectly. That would be a bit of a stretch. You know what? Why don't we ask her ourselves? If she denies it, we know what that means."

The gang then left for their residence. When they got there, they found Celia strolling around their gardens with a glass of red wine in one hand. They approached her.

"Mom, did you go to the station the last day?"

"Yes. I did. To understand the developments in the case."

They were almost too scared to ask, but they did anyway.

"Did you use the computer systems?"

Celia dodged the question. "And why do you care? Do you think I'm the one trying to kill you like your Uncle Jones? Because let me tell you something. He's delusional. That's it. And I think the police might just do a better job at finding out who the real killer is. Now please excuse me."

She walked off and into the house.

At that moment they knew that Celia had indeed tampered with the system. But what perplexed Bella, was why she didn't delete the footage. She could've done that and could've easily avoided that situation. She went to Jones with this.

He said, "There's something about narcissists. They always want to be identified. They crave attention, irrespective of whether it pertains to good, or bad things. Who knows, Celia might just have been one right from the start. She was awfully proud of herself. Always. Maybe that's the answer you need to get for now."

Every time Bella talked to her Uncle, nothing but doubt would still persist in her mind. She knew that he was hiding something, but couldn't talk to him about it. She couldn't talk to him about the chain of texts that she had been receiving from MANONYMOUS either.

Chapter 15

Family

Family is one of the only entities apart from friends, that can make you vulnerable. Family can lock eyes with you, and they can see right through. This is true in the case of some friendships too, but it isn't applicable, as not many keep secrets from friends. But in the context of family, there will always be skeletons in the closet of your mind. Basically, a vortex of secrets churning in your mind, causing turbulence. This is most ironic, because these skeletons in your closet, that are supposed to be made obscure, may seem too lucid to your family. The turbulence caused, may actually declutter and clear a few things, for your family. This is because these skeletons are supposed to be hidden from them. Some things that they should never come to know about. But reverse reactions do take place, making it so very clear to them.

The aforementioned thoughts were the skeletons in Jones' closet. Keeping secrets from his family. In all fairness, he didn't have any choice. But this was unbeknown to the others. Even Bella.

Probably playing his final card, Jones called a family meeting. He also asked Bella's friends, their parents, and Davies to attend the meeting at the den of the Throne residence. He knew what he had to say, but was worried. He would naturally be worried, because he was just about to give his family the benefit of the doubt, by finally letting them in on his plans.

It was about nightfall, when the Throne family, Davies, Bella and her gang, and all the parents concerned came together. They once again sat down unusually at their dinner table, which had the girth to fit more than 20 people. No one ate that night. Everyone probably figured that hearing bad news on an empty stomach might be better. None but Jones knew why they were to dine there. Celia was more than frustrated.

"Well, isn't anyone going to say anything at all? Are we just going to sit here all night? Can someone explain why we were asked to attend this charade?" said Celia, looking at Jones from the corner of her eye, in burgeoning anger.

Jones got up. He sighed and said, "Calm down, sister. You might be wondering why I asked you here. I did so, because my investigation has almost come to a close. I, right now, know why everything has been happening, and who is supposed to be held accountable for all of it."

Jones finished his sentence and looked around the room. He could see a few people with their mouths wide open. A few others made an effort to gulp back their surprise.

Jones said, "It's Celia."

Dr. Lodge and Mr. Throne looked horrified. They couldn't believe what they'd just heard. Lodge could barely speak. Mr. Throne roared, "That's it. You've crossed the line. We should never have welcomed you here after everything that you did. Celia didn't create problems about your staying here, and you raise such a ruckus here? This is nothing but a scandal!"

Celia scoffed, "Relax, Rob. I'm not surprised in the least. I knew he would get there. I don't know what I do to people that they hate me to this extent, but I bet something's there. I'm not asking for any kind of proof. I'm sure he's got some. So Detective Jones, why don't you just cuff me and take me to the precinct or wherever you take psychopaths like me? Go on, I'm waiting."

Ansy almost teared up. She scolded Jones. "Johan, what do you think you're doing? How dare you do this again? I was ready to forgive you the first time you did this because I knew you were a good detective and had the potential to do the right thing. But why would you implode this family again?"

Celia added, "It's okay, Ansy. There's nothing left of this family in the first place. He burned us down to ashes seventeen years ago. Bella, now do you have something to say too? You are a budding detective too, am I right?"

Bella couldn't get words to come out of her mouth. But she spoke, while having a breakdown. "Ma, we do have fair reason to believe you're the-"

Celia teared up too. "Well, now then Johan, you've succeeded in turning my own daughter against me. You've won. Now please don't torment them even more. Take me away from them."

Jones sighed, "Celia won't be arrested. At least not until she's had a mental examination. We have proof that she has split personality disorder. She always did. We doubt that it's the disorder that made her do all she did."

Celia laughed out loud. "Wow! Isn't that just great? I'm not just a serial killer. I'm nuts too!"

As Jones and a few of his officials took Celia away, Bella couldn't cry. She tried to. But couldn't. Her own mother had tried to kill everyone in the family. Succeeded in killing Graham. She looked back into the house and saw Mr. Lodge weeping on the floor, shouting Graham's name. Her father couldn't even be there. It was shocking for everyone. But there was one more thing that kept Bella from crying or even feeling bad for her mother. She didn't think it was her mother. Although Jones claimed that she was a narcissist, and that's why she left the footage for them to come and see, she couldn't believe it. If she were responsible for all of this, and she had one more person to kill, she wouldn't just let Jones get to her. She's too clever to have forgotten about the footage too. And if she really was a narcissist, she would have wanted to claim that she successfully planned out the whole deal before she got arrested. She didn't. she was just heart-broken that even her own daughter thought that she was guilty of everything that happened. But Jones couldn't possibly be wrong. There was no way.

The day soon came to a close. The next day, everyone was leaving. Lodge and his wife, having nothing else to do in life, decided to move someplace else. Bella's friends' parents left. But her friends decided to stay for Bella. Ansy and her husband decided to stay for a few more days, to help Bella and her father cope. Holly stayed too, as she was obligated to look after Bella's Nana. Jones and Davies were still at work. Finishing up.

Chapter 16

Death Day

Time goes on forever. It doesn't stop. Not even for a brief hiatus. But people die. And death doesn't necessarily have to be restricted to people. Events die too. And many, wait for the end of such dark events. It might happen during mysterious times, in unexpected settings.

Bella woke up, thinking that her Mom's face will be pasted across every one of the news channels and papers. MANONYMOUS. Someone who was feared by the entire town. Bella's mother. But surprisingly, she didn't find anything on any social media platform, newspapers, nor channels, except for the occasional small-time thefts, political developments, and so on. She didn't know what to think. Should she be relieved? Or should Bella think about why a deadly serial killer didn't catch the media's interest? She was too tired to think about anything at all.

Half past 10 in the morning, Mr. Throne left for running a few important errands. The kind which needs to be done when a member of one's family gets arrested for serial murder.

Holly was nursing Bella's Nana at the topmost floor of the house, while Mr. Umnom, who was seemingly indifferent to anything that happened in the house, was laughing away as he watched a sitcom on TV. Ansy was looking at old albums of herself and her siblings. They used to be so happy. Celia, Johan, and Ansy. What changed? No one knew. Why would a happy person like Celia turn out as a psychotic serial killer who wanted to hunt down her own family? At that moment, Bella and her friends walked in.

Ansy hid her tears and said, "Hi dear, do you want anything to eat?"

"No, Auntie. I'm actually confused. Why would my Mom do all this? What did she think she'd gain?"

"Bella, I don't have the answers you want. I've been thinking about it. Like Johan said, it might be a mental disorder that made her all narcissistic. We shouldn't trifle with Johan's findings. Everyone including me thought he was wrong the first time, but….." Ansy didn't complete her sentence. She sipped her tea, and asked her husband, "Jake, don't forget your meds. They're in your room."

Mr. Umnom sulked like a child, and went upstairs. Ansy, who felt responsible for Bella then on, asked Holly to prepare the table for lunch. She asked Bella's friends to come too. Bella hesitated. She didn't feel like eating.

"Bella dear, I know that this is all too much for absolutely anyone to handle. Know that I'm here for you. I'll stay here as long as you need me. Your Uncle Jake is an idiot, as you know. Don't mind him. He's always been that way. Now you kids come and eat something. No need to wait for Jake.

I'm sure he has already stuffed himself with the maximum of his capabilities."

They sat down to eat. Holly had cooked them a scrumptious meal. They started eating. For some reason, Bella kept looking away from her plate and to her friends' faces. They looked back with gestures, asking what's up. Bella clenched her fists, as if preparing for something. She asked, "Auntie, how do you know about it?"

"Know about what, dear?"

"Uncle Jones told only me about the fact that Ma could be narcissistic. Earlier you said the same thing."

"I was just guessing, dear."

"Oh, alright."

Bella quietly took out her phone under the table, and started to text Jones and Davies.

Ansy smiled, "Oh, there's no need to text anyone, dear. No one's coming."

Bella understood their situation by that time. But her friends were still puzzled. Jay whispered to Bella, "Bella, what the hell is going on?"

Ansy replied to that, "Oh dear God, these kids….. Even without beating about the bush this time, they just don't get it, do they?"

They got up hastily. Bella called out to Holly. She came running, and said, "Ansy, please leave them alone. You've already caused enough problems. You even got Celia in jail. Wasn't that what you wanted? To not get caught? Now please, I beg you. Stop."

Ansy laughed like the psychopath she was. "Holly, it's like you've never known me. Now the world believes that Celia did all this, when the truth is, that this is all my hard work and skill. I want them to know that. I want to be appreciated for once in my life!"

Bella stared at her in utter disbelief. "You wanted attention, so what, you just decided to become a serial killer? For 17 years?"

Ansy laughed again. "Oh my God Bella! You're unbelievable. I didn't want attention. I never have. Okay, clearly you guys don't get what's happening, no matter how many hints I've given. Story time, it is then!"

Suddenly she got all grave and emotional. "17 years ago, I was in college. That's when our family business started going downhill. We were always the strongest businessmen and women, but our partners traded our personal business up for another big company. They also took away the money from the joint accounts by faking every document. They were just cruel, cut-throats. Mom and Dad panicked a lot. They resorted to accepting bribes themselves to support the family. They were always honest to a fault. But they had to. Otherwise, we would have been bankrupt. They were miserable. They had to do things that they never dreamed of doing, to support us. They asked Johan and Celia for help. They never asked me. I had already started my business back then too. I had a lot of money saved up. But my parents never expected me to. I even offered. They just acted surprised and didn't take my money. Everyone always thought I wasn't capable of anything. That I was a very quiet, introverted person who lives by, mooching off the rich family. Even you kids. You never even considered me a suspect. You even proceeded to suspect that some redhead was hired to do the job of framing Celia, rather than trying to comprehend that this redhead was more than capable. It either screams out the way you think of me or it just shows how capable I am. It's a win-win. Truth be told, the last 17 years is a testament to the fact that I'm the most capable of us all."

Bella couldn't believe her ears. "Are you out of your mind? You killed my friend, made us and our families miserable for days, if not weeks, and that too, all just to prove your stupid point?"

"Bella Bella Bella, let me finish. And don't even start with your friend. He was just roadkill. The assistant man too. That's why I didn't use canvases in either of their cases. I had to get to the island on a boat to kill Claudius McKinsley and I see some kid swimming up to the shore. What else was I supposed to do? To continue, I figured that they'd never ask for my help. They thought I was meek and incapable. They even told me that."

Bella was about to fly off the handle. She couldn't stand to hear that her friend was just collateral damage caused by her Aunt's sinisterly unhinged revenge plot. But she had to keep listening. There was obviously something wrong with her. What if she had a weak point? Something that could trigger her? Bella immediately started calling her Uncle.

"Bella, trust me. He is not answering. Oh and I forgot to mention. Your Dad is either in the hospital or dead. A tiny car accident. Seriously, I hired to kill him off, but how much can you trust private services right? Especially when the guy I hired to kill that fool of a businessman Goldson is right now hanging by some tree. The guy apparently couldn't live with himself after killing someone. These privately hired guys I'm telling you. Complete fools!"

Bella didn't give up. She couldn't .She played her last card. "You do realize Uncle Jones knows about all this? Yea, that's right. I texted him right when I understood that you were behind all this. He said he's coming with the full force."

Ansy laughed like the maniac she was. "Oh! Bella, I hadn't thought of that! You texted this phone right?"

She held out Jones' iPhone.

"That's right. I took it out of his pocket when I hugged him when he felt bad about Celia being arrested."

Bella didn't know what to do next. All her friends stared at her, hoping that she knew what to do next. Jay understood that Bella didn't, and knew that she needed time. By that time, he knew that Bella's aunt is a narcissist, and figured out that it'd be easy to stall. He said, "So wait, are you MANONYMOUS?"

"Oh yes, I forgot about that part. Yes, I am. Seriously, personally I thought that the name MANONYMOUS was a big giveaway. I thought that you guys would figure it out right at the start. But then again, no one expects me to do anything, ergo here we are. It's an anagram, idiots! MANONYMOUS for ANSY O. UMNOM. That's the name I fed to Goldson and that assistant of his, another idiotic partner of mine. The man was corrupt too. I may have kind of pretended to want to help Goldson in their plans to crush their rival's empire illegally, but actually, what I wanted was to take Goldson away to plan and kill him. And I asked him to rent out his Manor to some people, who happened to be you kids, under my name."

Their horror could not possibly be put into words. The chill that ran down everyone's spine could be equated to a metro train. Ansy was certainly brilliant. But what she did.....she killed her enemies just to prove that she's capable of just about anything. She recognized her strengths by killing people and by gaslighting her family. And now the rest of Bella's sane family was going to be dead. She too will be, probably. But....

She shouted at Ansy. "A true serial killer would have killed only according to their M.O. But you're waiting for the last kill now. It's not Mr. Lodge. His partners were corrupt. He wasn't. You wouldn't kill Holly. And my mother was just the resource you needed to frame so that I wouldn't figure out that it's you soon. Dad isn't like that either. So your last kill has to be-"

Ansy interrupted. "Right you are, Bella. Your Nana. My mother. And yes, that's the other reason why I had to continue my escapade for another 17 years. It was worth it. She conned my father into signing business deals with those people. I said she was honest, like my Dad. My Dad thought so, and he died believing so. That's why I still claimed that your Nana did honest business. But she was corrupt too. And I found out after doing some research on my family's dealings because they wouldn't tell me themselves."

"So, Ma and Uncle Jones knew?"

"Yes. Johan didn't care about the technicalities as it didn't matter to him. And Celia selfishly supported it because she needed the money for her own business. I was the only one who saw our father's heart break. And that was when I decided that I'll avenge him, by punishing everyone responsible for his death. Including Johan and Celia. I framed Celia because she was selfish, and helped ruin my Dad's business for money. And Johan never cared. He'd just run away from all his problems. So , I decided to punish him for his indifference, by letting him see the death of people he cares about drawing closer and closer till he snapped. So that he can feel pain and concern for once in his life. And this is the final segment of my plan. The closure. The death day. I revealed myself before you, and let you find out the truth, because one, I wanted to prove that you could never outrun me, and two, because I want everyone to know why I did what I did. Why they suffered for 17 whole years. I want them to live with that pain. I killed the rest of the parties involved because they didn't deserve it. That's how I abided by my M.O. I think my job here is done."

After saying that, she immediately reached out for the pistol in her pocket and went upstairs to Nana Throne's room.

Holly stopped her.

"You can't blackmail me anymore. I won't let you spill one more drop of blood. You are done. I know you won't kill me. You are not my Ansy. You are the devil that possessed her. You are the witch that ruined the family. My old, sweet Ansy is gone. You killed her."

Ansy pushed old Holly out of her way.

"I was able to black-mail you about you unknowingly giving me Celia's old canvases, Holly. But believe me, Holly, I've only had love for you. You are probably the only one left in this household, that I still love. And Bella of course. My darling Bella. But for the record, her admiration for Johan was just annoying."

Bella cut in between. "All you want is here. Leave my friends. They don't mean anything to you."

Ansy chuckled. "You're right, Bella. They have always been just roadkill to me. Lodge invited your friends to tag along, not me. Let him take the blame for whatever. And what I gained from it? I didn't have to hurt you but I had to keep you and your friends in the loop so that you wouldn't accidentally walk into any of my well-planned schemes. But since that was a complete bust, here we are now! I'm your only family now, Bella. You wouldn't implode that, now would you? So stop blaming things on me and appreciate the fact that you are loved and listened to, for once in your life."

Saying this, Ansy stormed into her mother's room. Bella and her friends couldn't move. Holly couldn't stop her. She wanted this to end. She thought to herself, "I have to save Bella, at least. This is the least I can do after enabling Ansy. If she kills Nana Throne, she will probably leave the children alone."

She didn't move. In fact, no one did. It wasn't that they hated Nana. It was just fear. Fear of Ansy's next possible move. Fear, that if they don't let Ansy proceed with it, she'll continue the charade for another 17 years. They could never live with that thought.

And so they waited. And waited. Waiting to hear a gunshot from Nana's room. Anticipating the worst.

Thinking about fate, destiny, and other such philosophical thoughts. What would happen after death? What would be waiting for them at the end of time? Why were they in that particular situation in life? They had the weirdest moment in their whole life. Ironic, because by that time, they were not far from being lifeless.

But even after much waiting, they heard no gunshot. No haunting, traumatizing screams. Just silence. The same screeching silence that one usually experiences in a dark room in a horror movie of mediocre standards. Bella suspected the arrival of something even more sinister by then. She, along with her friends rushed, leaving the frozen Holly, only to find an unexpectedly familiar face upstairs in Nana's room. There, they saw their fate turn. Jones was holding Ansy at gunpoint.

After a moment of silence, Bella and the rest finally came to their senses. Except for the bedridden Nana of course. And then Jones gave out his signature sigh. The one that he usually gives out before giving a lengthy speech.

"Didn't expect me here did you?"

Ansy was speechless. Well, in fairness, what could she say, really?

"You thought you had me there, when you swiped my phone. But I knew you'd try to tie up all loose ends. I wanted you to take my phone. Yeah. I bugged my own phone. I knew you'd try something like that. I pretended to have a breakdown, thus giving you the perfect opportunity. I had your puerile MANONYMOUS anagram all figured out long back. I had a hunch that it was you, the moment you mentioned The Artist when you came here.

Another charade of yours. Like you were giving me a bone, just like when you gave me that boat so that we could get back so that you could finish what you started. I just said there were serial murders. But you, being your egoistic self, wanted me to catch a hint, and immediately suggested your previous alias. You sent your company's labourers to kill Graham and Goldston, without Jake knowing. Not that he'd stop you if he knew. You tried to frame Celia for 17 years."

Bella had other doubts in her mind, although that speech was much revealing.

"But, we saw Mom on the surveillance camera visuals."

"Credits to your Aunt, yet again. I presume she persuaded Celia to go to the station, maybe to discuss business with Davies, who also happens to be her business partner. After entering the station with your Mom, she must've waited outside and asked for access to the security's computer. Since she went with Celia, they obviously gave her special Throne privileges. And then she must've cropped out the rest of the footage."

Ansy nodded in agreement. It was almost as if she was happy that everyone identified her as The Artist and MANONYMOUS. Both her alter-egos. As if she was given "credit".

Jones continued. "I knew about all this long back. But I had to put up a rather unconfident facade, so that I could bring out Ansy's well-known egoism and narcissistic tendencies. I apologize, Bella, for keeping all this from you. I had to make sure everyone except you was out of the house somehow. I needed you here to keep Ansy engaged in her self-absorption, and to figure things out on your own. And sister, the police will be here any minute. I've asked Davies to follow me here."

Ansy pulled her fits of laughter again.

"Dear brother, you really think I haven't thought this through? You think I'd just give you tell-tale signs myself, without a plan? How you underestimate me! Even now. That's what is so incredible. I've already mixed something in our dear Momma's porridge. And do you remember brother, we used to jump out of this very window and climb onto that tree. That's one of the only childhood memories I've cherished. Away from Mom. Just me, you, and Celia. And you know, the window is still big enough."

Everyone looked at each other with perplexed faces. And then it suddenly clicked. That was when Ansy jumped from the window, and Nana's monitor's ECG waves turned flat, with a beep.

And there it ended. There wouldn't be another resurrection. Some screamed. Some froze. They couldn't bear to look down.

Jones spoke, "Goodbye, Ansy. You completed your mission. You took our mother with you. You died, feeling credited. Good for you."

That was basically it. Celia was dropped back home. They had explained everything to her on the way. Maybe that's why she was in tears when she returned. Bella's Dad was recovering at the hospital. Ansy was taken in a bodybag. Bella's Nana too. Of course, they had to do a lot of explaining for Jake. Bella went to see her friends off, as their parents rushed in, to take them home. Other than that, was that family fine?

Not a chance. They were far from fine. It could be said that the family was "under re-construction".

The family stood outside, blankly staring at the wailing police vehicles and ambulances. Everything and everyone glowed in the darkness of the night and of their state of mind. The neighbours stared in silence. The media shouted in the pitch of sirens. In their fairness, the esteemed Throne family's dark secrets and mysteries were out.

Celia walked up to Jones. It was the first time she initiated a proper conversion between them. "Jo..Johan, did you know 17 years back?"

"No. I regretted suspecting one sister. Couldn't hazard the other. I'm sorry. I've only given you trouble, the past seventeen years. It's time I move away for real."

"Stay. You saved my daughter. Hell, you saved this town. And I don't want to put the past between us anymore. I only have you to talk to, after Bella leaves for college. I missed you all these years, Johan. And now, I know most of the rifts between us were not your fault. I want you here. Bella wants you here. Stay."

Although that moment was certainly meaningful, happiness still didn't start showering. It wasn't time yet. But eventually it will be. The cliched adage would hopefully work in their favour. Everything will return to the so-called 'normal'. All they had to do was wait. Maybe another seventeen years. Who knows? Nothing remains cold forever. Eventually, everything recedes. Like a flight of stairs.

www.ingramcontent.com/pod-product-compliance
Ingram Content Group UK Ltd.
Pitfield, Milton Keynes, MK11 3LW, UK
UKHW021935190726
13853UKWH00004B/1462

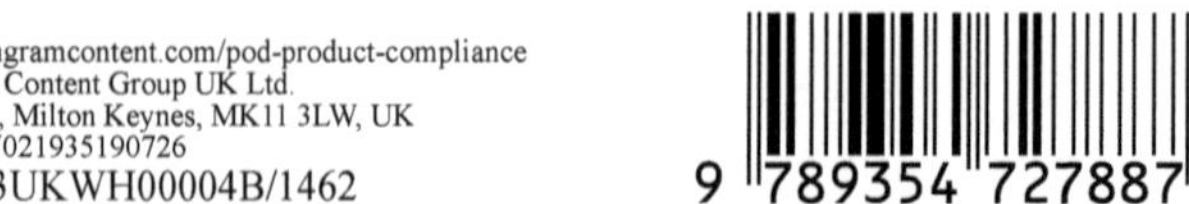

9 789354 727887